Chasing

Rain

~A NOVEL~

Elizabeth James

Romance on the Boardwalk Series

Book #2

Edited by Kathy Krick

Cover by ShamRock Cover
Designs ©2014

DEDICATION

Once again, at publishing time, I find myself thinking of Sissy and Bobby who would've loved every minute of my journey as an author. Sissy would have been right beside me, giving me feedback and encouragement and Bobby would've just said "That's cool!" Years have passed but it seems like just yesterday I had to say goodbye. I love you both and know you're with me every step of the way. ~with all my love

THANK YOU

To my husband for putting up with this crazy world I've gotten myself into. I appreciate your support and hope one day you'll actually read one of my books! I love you!

Thanks again to my mom and dad for being an amazing support for me my entire life and for giving me a wonderful example of life-long love. I love you both! And thank you to my family for being a pretty awesome bunch! I love you all too!!

To my "sisters", I love you all and thank you for encouraging me to keep on with my dream!

To Kassie Baker who knows me better than I know myself sometimes, thank you! You've been an amazing friend and "assistant" for all five books now!

WOW…and yet you still haven't killed me. Miracles do happen!

Kathy Krick, thank you again. You have always given me the feedback I need to keep my thoughts together and you always find my boo boos. You rock!

To Rochelle who has captured Averi and Ian on the cover and brought them to life. Thank you for your talent!!

To my beta readers: Kassie Baker, Jodi Negri, Maria DeSouza, Becky Nichols and Sharon Courtney…thank you again for your amazing input and suggestions. I hope you like the finished product!

To my fellow authors in FTLOF, thank you for all of your support and I'm so happy to have finally met some of you in person!

To my E. James Street Team: Thank you for all of your support and encouragement throughout the past year, I love each and every one of you.

Prologue

Averi

My grandpa always said, 'A leopard can't change his spots.' He would've said the same thing about Ian O'Neal. Just when I thought he'd finally grown up and realized he needed to settle down, he'd shown his true colors, once again. Things had been going great. We'd been spending a lot of time together while watching over my best friend Kendall, who'd been wrapped up in a huge mess involving two very dangerous guys, and during that time, I'd seen a glimmer of hope for the two of us. Since I had to work and he was working whenever he wanted to, he volunteered to hang out with her at the coffee shop as undercover security and report back to me, which he did every evening. I'd always had a crush on him, but we never spent any one on one time together. Over pizza and beer, we joked, we flirted and most of all, became really close friends. Spending that time together made me realize how strong my feelings really were for him. The butterflies in my stomach every time I saw him and the way I couldn't quite catch my breath when he was near, were signs that I had it bad, real bad. I began to believe he'd changed, until the night he ripped my heart apart.

It happened only a few days after Kendall and Tristan's engagement. Ian stopped by my shop, as he usually did and mentioned that he was going to hang out down at the Fat Pelican and even suggested that I come by. After closing for the day and throwing on a cute sundress, I dashed to the bar only to walk in and find him wrapped in another woman's arms. At first, I couldn't believe what I was seeing, but it was pretty obvious something was going on. Numbly, I retraced my steps and once outside, had to lean against the wall to stop myself from swaying. He never saw me, but the vision I had in my head just wouldn't go away. With tears of anger burning my eyes, I wiped them away with my palms then stumbled to my Jeep. Once inside, I dropped my forehead against the steering wheel, but every time I closed my eyes, I could see them together, her lips just a breath away from his neck.

Cranking my Jeep, I threw it in gear and with squealing tires, I pulled away from the curb. I'd only gone a few miles when the tears threatened to spill again so I pulled into a deserted public beach access, parked and shut off my motor.

"WHY?" I screamed, my voice choked with emotion. "Why does he have to be such a jerk? Why do I still give a damn?"

Sobbing, I slammed my fists onto the steering wheel.

"Umm, are you okay?" I heard a male voice behind me and immediately my heart jumped into my throat. I whipped my head around to see a man in a uniform standing next to my door.

Instantly, relief flooded over me. "Oh, I'm sorry, officer. I just needed a place to compose myself. It was safer than trying to drive." I wiped the tears from my cheeks with the back of my hand, then fished a tissue out of my purse and blew my nose.

He stepped closer and smiled. "I'm not a cop," he chuckled. "I work at the fire station down the road."

Upon closer inspection of his uniform, I could see the difference and I laughed. "Oh well, color me embarrassed. I guess you get that a lot." He was my age, tall, blonde, blue-eyed and very good looking.

He smiled, revealing impossibly white teeth and shrugged his broad shoulders. "It's all good. So, back to you...are you okay?"

After taking a deep breath, I returned the smile. "Yes, I will be. I'm sorry I worried you..." I looked at his name tag and saw *A. Reynolds.*

Following my gaze, he held out his hand and said, "Oh, sorry. I'm Alex...Alex Reynolds."

Shaking his hand firmly, I said, "Averi Rain. Nice to meet you."

He gave me the sweetest smile. Looking down at his watch, he said, "Well, Ms. Rain. I hope you'll have a better night. I need to get going, my shift is starting soon. I don't live far from here so I like to walk to work when the weather lets me." He indicated down the street where I could just make out the lights of the fire station.

I nodded and smiled. "I understand and I'm sorry I distracted you...and hey, you can call me Averi."

He started to back away, then stopped and said, "Averi...it was the best kind of distraction." He threw up his hand, turned and disappeared into the darkness.

I drove home and when I got there, I checked my phone. I'd missed a call from Ian. The voicemail said, "Hey, where are you?" I could hear giggling in the background, and the phone became muffled then disconnected.

The next morning, he'd shown up at my shop, but as fate would have it, so did Alex. He'd tracked me down through mutual friends and he and Ian practically walked into each other coming in the door. Still hurt and feeling vindictive, I'd been icy to Ian and overly warm to Alex. So warm, in fact, he invited me out to dinner and with a deliberate glare toward Ian, I immediately accepted. Like a whipped puppy, Ian quietly left and despite many more unanswered calls from him, I hadn't seen him until the rehearsal dinner for Tristan and Kendall's wedding. Alex and I had begun seeing each other casually, but of course, everyone assumed we were in a more serious relationship, and I didn't correct them. All that evening, Ian tried to corner me to talk, but I managed to avoid him and spent the evening hanging all over Alex. I was hurt and was going to make him suffer.

The next day, at the wedding, he tried desperately to make eye contact with me, but I kept my gaze averted as much as possible. I focused on Alex but felt Ian's eyes on me the entire time. Following a beautiful ceremony, the minister pronounced Tristan and Kendall, man and wife and I turned to watch them walk down the aisle. Alex had planned to escort me to the reception and my intentions, once again, were to cling to him. What I didn't expect was Ian holding out his arm for me saying what he did, so low only I could hear.

Hell went through me. My face flushed red, and I drew back my hand. With indignation, I said, "No, Ian...you're not."

He frowned and before I could react, he picked me up and threw me over his shoulder. He marched up the aisle with me kicking and screaming, and I saw a frowning Alex look around for a moment then get up to follow. Ian had a head start, however, and when we arrived at the tent where the reception was going to be held, he finally put me down. Breathlessly, he said, "Averi, I don't know what I've done to make you hate me but there's something I have to do."

I started to speak but felt his arms wrap around me, and his lips come down on mine. Immediately, I went limp in his arms and my lips suddenly had a mind of their own as I responded to his kiss. My mind was screaming 'What are you doing??' so I pushed him away. I quickly wiped my mouth with the back of my hand and hissed, "Are you crazy?"

He didn't seem fazed at all by my reaction. Instead, he cradled my chin with his fingers and tilted my head up to force my eyes to meet his. "I *am* crazy and I'm also sorry. I'm sorry for whatever caused you to run away from me. If you're happy then I'm man enough to step away but I'll always be close by. Just ask yourself if you're truly happy."

My mouth dropped open. I couldn't hide my surprise at his words. He left me speechless and dumbfounded. I watched him turn and quickly walk away. Stunned, I found tears welling in my eyes, and I blinked them back. Taking a deep breath, I closed my eyes and touched my fingers to my still tingling lips, and I felt a strange ache inside. The kiss I'd always dreamed of sharing with Ian had finally come, but not in the way I'd envisioned. A moment later, when I opened my eyes, I found Alex standing in front of me, questions in his eyes. "Are you okay? What in the hell just happened?"

I took a deep breath before answering. "What did you see?" My face was flushed with both excitement and embarrassment.

"What I saw was that guy Ian throw what I thought was *my* girlfriend over his shoulder…that's what I saw." He was visibly upset and honestly, I knew he had every right to be but inside, I was secretly relieved he hadn't seen the kiss.

My voice sounded weird as I tried to be as normal as possible. "Well, he's like a brother to me and he thought he was being funny. Obviously, he wasn't," I said, forcing a laugh. "He's such a dork."

An awkward silence followed, then he gave me half a smile. "Well, you looked upset when I came in…are you sure you're okay?" He trailed his fingertips down my flushed cheek.

At his touch, once again, that fake laughed popped out. "Oh sure, I was just upset because I thought he'd messed up my dress. It's all good." Why was I lying? Lying to Alex was becoming easy and that made me nauseous. Why couldn't I just tell him the truth?

He smiled, kissed me on the forehead and then held out his hand. "Well, would you come dance with me? I want to be the only one holding you tonight." I could hear the music cranking up as the guests arrived.

Nodding with a smile, I put my hand in his. "I'd be honored."

I hadn't seen Ian since, and I hated to admit, it was killing me.

Chapter 1

Averi

"He's an ass!"

I threw my backpack down on the table causing the coffee cups to teeter precariously but miraculously, nothing spilled. I plopped down in the chair and looked up to find Kendall staring at me with her mouth wide open.

"Averi, there are customers in here," she whispered while glancing around to see if anyone was watching.

Loudly, I said, "Well, if they know Ian O'Neal then they know I speak the truth!" I looked around to see several customers look up from their book/coffee morning fix and was actually rewarded with a couple of nods and knowing smiles, and I had to chuckle. Out of respect for my best friend, I did lower my voice, but still couldn't contain my irritation. "Kendall, you've been gone on your honeymoon and it's been killing me that I haven't been able to give you the lowdown on what he did after the wedding. Do you know he had the nerve, as we got ready to walk back down the aisle, to hold out his arm and say in front of everyone, 'You know *I am* the best man?!' I don't think Alex heard him but then he tossed me over his shoulder and carried me away like a sack of potatoes!"

Kendall sat down across from me, her lips scrunched to keep from laughing so I poked her. "What! I'm not laughing," she said, tears forming in the corners of her eyes. "I can only imagine how mad you were." A giggle escaped, but she quickly clamped her lips shut.

Tapping my foot like a mad woman, I whispered, "Mad? Mad isn't the word. Furious? Getting closer. He's so cocky and arrogant. Does he think all he has to do is look my way and I'll melt into his arms? I've moved on and Alex suits me just fine!"

Kendall's eyes narrowed as she leaned closer to me. "Are you sure about that? I know you've had a thing for Ian for years. Are you telling me that you can just turn it on and off...just like that?" She snapped her fingers to emphasize her point, and I had to turn away. Kendall could read me like a book, and I didn't want to have to explain that it wasn't too hard to do once you've caught someone with another woman. Again, I replayed that night in my mind and came to the same conclusion. He was an ass!

"Earth to Averi," I heard Kendall say. I looked up over to see her waving her hand in front of my face. "Where did you go? You suddenly spaced out when I asked you about Ian."

Not realizing I'd done that, I laughed. Recovering quickly, I changed the subject. "Oh sorry, I was just thinking that I'm such a selfish friend. Instead of whining to you about Ian, I should've been asking about your honeymoon. Was it all kinds of wonderful? I've never been to the Bahamas but I hear it's gorgeous."

She pursed her lips studying my face. "Hmm, I noticed you just changed the subject, by the way, and I'll let it slide for now but only because I've got tons to tell you!" She jumped up from her chair, walked over to the counter, reaching behind it, she brought out a polka-dotted gift bag. "I got you something from our trip and as soon as I saw it, I thought of you."

"Um, Kendall. You actually left your hotel room long enough to do some shopping?" I said laughing as she sat the bag in front of me.

She sat back down and pushed the bag across the table toward me. "You're funny. Actually, we were hardly in our room. We went snorkeling, which I loved, by the way, and parasailing...which I didn't love so much. You know how easily I burn so I slathered myself in sunblock to be able to do all those outdoorsy things. My gorgeous husband just got darker and darker. One evening, after dinner, we went to the local market and I told Tristan that I just had to find a perfect gift for you and this is what I found." She pointed again to the brightly colored bag brimming with matching tissue paper.

I started to open it, but stopped and with a straight face said, "I've always wanted a gift bag. Thank you so much."

"Hardy har...open the damn bag," she said, crossing her arms as she leaned back in the chair. "You make things so difficult!" She laughed.

Reaching in, I carefully pulled the paper free to find a tiny package wrapped with a silver bow. She smiled, watching me closely. I untied the bow, opened it and the moment I glanced inside, I gasped. Nestled in the satin lining was a beautiful pink pearl pendant on a delicate silver chain. I gently lifted the necklace from the box and watched as the light danced across its smooth surface. "It's breathtaking! Kendall, this is too much!"

She smiled brightly as she took the necklace from me to fasten it around my neck. "I never got to give you a Maid of Honor gift so this is my thanks to you for all you did to make my wedding day so perfect."

I felt the cold pearl against my skin and reached up to touch it gently. "Thank you so much for being my friend and I was honored to be a part of your big day," I said standing up to hug her tightly. "I love you, my friend."

"Besties to the end, right?" She hugged me back as I nodded and smiled. We sat back down, and I listened as she recounted their trip of a lifetime, but I found my mind drifting away to Ian. Why couldn't I stop thinking of him? He was as frustrating as hell, but for some reason, I was drawn to him. Obviously, my common sense was broken, or at least warped. Ian was trouble with a capital T and the saddest part was I knew in my heart that a future with him wasn't possible.

Kendall's phone chimed interrupting the description of her now infamous parasailing incident where the top half of her bikini popped off as she sailed over the crystal blue water. Holding up her finger, she said, "Oh, it's Tristan. Let me get this." She answered and immediately, her voice softened. "Hey baby…I miss you too…yeah, I'm talking to Averi." She paused then smiled. "Oh, she loved it! I knew she would." Her voice dropped to a whisper, but I could still make out her saying, "No, I don't think she's seen him."

I picked up my bag and my phone and waved to get her attention. *"I'm going,"* I mouthed. She nodded, then gave me another tight hug. I walked to the door, glanced back and saw a glowing woman in love as she talked to her husband. Was I happy for her? Yes, of course. Was I jealous? Sure. My only hope was to give my relationship with Alex a chance and leave Ian behind. He really was a nice guy and had been a perfect gentleman.

When I got home, I found the front door unlocked. Normally, my parents were never home, but tonight they were. Technically, I lived at home, but in reality rented a loft apartment above the garage. My mom and dad were sitting in the den when I walked in.

"Averi! We're glad you're home," my mom said, standing to give me a kiss on the cheek. "Sit down, we've got something to talk to you about."

I flopped onto the couch, kicked my flip flops off and dropped my gift bag and keys on the floor beside me. "If this is about my dirty laundry in the apartment, I promise I'll catch up. It's been a crazy week."

My mom screwed up her face. "Laundry? Oh no, that's not what we want to talk about…but now that you mention it, you'd better get that taken care of." She looked at my dad and nodded slightly.

My dad cleared his throat nervously. "Baby girl, I have great news! I got the promotion at the plant."

I sat up straight and smiled. "Daddy! That's great! I'm so happy for you!" There was an awkward silence as they looked at each other not saying anything. Something was up. "What's going on?" I asked warily.

"Well, honey," my mom began, "your dad's promotion means we have to relocate. We're going to be moving to Boone."

I jumped up from the couch. "Boone?! That's like fifteen hours from here!" I cried. "Why do you have to go there?"

My mom laughed. "Averi, stop being so dramatic. It's only a little over five hours to Boone."

My dad put his hand on hers. "Baby girl, this is a big move for me. I'll be the district manager for the entire east coast and the headquarters are there. I can't stay here to do what I need to do. You know it's always been my dream."

I found myself whining and I hated myself for it but for some reason, couldn't stop. "But if you leave, I won't be able to live here. You guys rent the house now and I know I won't be able to afford it on my own." I fell back on the couch. "How long do I have before you leave?" I said panic in my voice.

They exchanged worried glances. Finally, my mom spoke in a rush, "We leave in two weeks."

"Two weeks?" I closed my eyes. "How am I going to find somewhere to live in that short amount of time?"

I felt my mom's hand on mine. "Honey, I know this is out of the blue but you're a grown woman now and we know you'll be fine. Our friend Sharilyn, who's in real estate, is looking for apartments for you."

I groaned. "Mom, I'm trying not to freak out but…I'm totally freaking out." I turned to my dad. "I'm happy for you, Daddy. Really, I am. I just don't know what I'll do!" My stomach was in knots thinking about them leaving.

My dad pulled out his checkbook. "Averi, we know you're not financially prepared to shell out deposits and things so I'll give you enough to get you started. We don't want to leave you homeless." He wrote out a check and handed it to me, and as I stared down at it, I felt tears spring to my eyes.

"Daddy, I can't take that. I've got some money put aside that I can use. I'm gonna have to learn to do this on my own and now's as good a time as any to start." Taking a deep breath, I pushed his hand back. "Thank you, but no thank you."

His brows furrowed. "You *will* take this, just consider it to be your birthday and Christmas all in one if that'll make it easier to take. Please, honey. Let us do this for you."

Reluctantly, I took the check, but I vowed to myself to pay them back as soon as I could. My mom smiled and said, "Averi, you'll land on your feet. You always do. We have faith in you, sweetie." My parents were awesome and so supportive, and I was so blessed to have them. They'd been so wonderful to Kendall when her parents and younger sister had been lost in a tragic fire, taking her in as if she was one of their own. It was only recently that we'd learned that the fire had been started accidentally by one of

Kendall's former friends, Sebastian Cole. Thankfully, he'd left town after confessing the truth to her and hadn't been seen since. His sidekick, Logan, had ended up in jail for possession of performance enhancing drugs. He was now in Central Prison in Raleigh and the word going around was that he'd found out the hard way that he wasn't so tough after all.

Getting up from the couch, I hugged my parents and climbed the stairs to my apartment. As I walked in the door, my eyes scanned my sparsely furnished place, and I realized I'd just been hanging out here, this wasn't a home. Time to grow up! Yay, me! I threw my keys on the counter, then plopped down on my futon, turned on my laptop and started searching for apartments. Right away, I realized this was not going to be an easy feat in a beachfront community. Most rentals in the area were targeting families coming down to the beach for vacation. They weren't going to be interested in renting for a reasonable monthly rate when they could get weekly rent for four times that. Dejected and sick to my stomach, I closed my laptop, curled into a ball and cried myself to sleep.

Chapter 2

Ian

I crept from my room just after sunrise, careful not to make too much noise. Tristan and Kendall were still asleep, and I needed to get to the beach early so I could start my lifeguarding shift. It was Saturday morning and not having to wear the suit and tie was a sweet relief. I was finding out real quick that being a responsible adult was not all it was cracked up to be. I was looking forward to being out on the beach in the sun, breathing in the fresh sea breeze and also was hoping to catch a glimpse of Averi when she opened her shop. She'd been avoiding me, and I had no clue why. The last time I'd talked to her, I'd invited her to meet at the Fat Pelican, but she'd never showed. My texts and calls had gone unanswered, so I decided the next logical step would be to talk to her in person. Unfortunately, some fireman joker showed up at the same time and he did what I wasn't able to do, get a date with her. I'd replayed the events preceding the anti-Ian campaign, but couldn't put my finger on what I'd done. I'd tried to find out from Kendall, but she was as confused as I was telling me just to give her time. Finally, I decided to pull her aside at the wedding to get her alone to talk, but once again, my big mouth had to ruin it. Actually, the moment I said the words, "I AM the best man" her face clouded over, and I knew I'd screwed up. She'd stood immobile and with a clenched jaw, refused to take my arm. Confused, frustrated *and* without thinking, I'd scooped her up and had her over my shoulder before I knew it. My plan was to get her alone and when I arrived with her at the still deserted reception tent, I knew I only had moments to say what I wanted before the guests arrived. Having her this close was more than I could stand. I did what I'd been wanting to for years. Pulling her close, I held her soft body tightly in my arms, her lips only a breath from mine. When she didn't resist, I kissed her. The taste of her lips was sweeter than I'd ever dreamed and when she parted them for me, I lost my breath for a moment. Her body went limp in my arms. The world stood completely still, and I truly didn't want it to end.

A few moments passed, then it was almost as if someone threw cold water on her. She suddenly stiffened in my arms, like she was coming to her senses. Eyes narrowed, she glared at me, and I could tell she was furious. Time was running out to speak my peace, so I did. Cradling her chin in my palm, I had to force her to look at me because I wanted her to see the sincerity in my eyes. My words had been unscripted and heartfelt and tumbled out in a rush. When I finished, she seemed surprised for a moment giving me a little hope but then her anger took over again. Her eyes shifted behind me and grew wide and when I turned, I could see Alex approaching the tent, so I just left, knowing I'd done all I could to let her know how I felt. I hadn't been able to speak to her since, only stealing glimpses of her on the boardwalk and getting random updates from Kendall.

Distracted by my thoughts, I suddenly realized if I didn't hustle, I was going to be late. I checked the clock as I turned on the kitchen light to get some juice from the fridge, and I noticed some pictures held by magnets on the door. They were from Tristan and Kendall's honeymoon, and I could see they were truly and completely happy. It was then I noticed that Kendall had been putting her feminine touches on the place, and it was really looking great. As I stood there taking in all the changes, it hit me. This was their home now. My living here was invading their privacy, and even though I knew my brother would never put me out on the street, I needed to find another place to crash. I left the house determined to find a home of my own as soon as possible.

My day turned out to be pretty exciting since I'd spent most of the day searching for a missing kid, who finally turned up about a mile down the beach. I found him sitting on an empty blanket eating a sandwich he'd taken from someone's cooler. After a tearful reunion with his parents and a lecture from me about wandering off, I dragged myself to my truck then headed over to Mom's house. I wanted to talk to her about possibly staying with her for a while *and* snag some awesome home cooking in the process.

Mom unfortunately gave me bad news. "Oh Ian, you know I'd love for you to stay with me but your aunt Lucinda is coming in from Nevada this week and she's going to be using the guest room. Since she and your uncle Jim split up, she's been planning to start over fresh in a new town. With your dad gone, I've been lonely and this seemed to be the best solution for us both. You're more than welcome to sleep on the couch though, if you need somewhere to stay," she said as we finished our dinner.

Shaking my head, I laughed. "No, Mom. I'll be okay. I just thought you might need me to keep you company. I'm fine over at Tristan's. I'll just save up some more money then get my own place."

She hugged me tightly. "I'm so proud of how responsible you've become since your dad passed away. He would have been so proud of you."

Every time I thought about my dad, I got teary eyed. He'd recently lost his battle with cancer, and I missed him like crazy. Looking back, I regretted that I'd been such a screw up while he'd been alive. He spoke with me in his hospital room right before he died telling me he loved me and was proud of me, but I knew in my heart, he'd always wished I'd done better for myself. Tristan was the golden child who'd always succeeded, and I'd always felt lost in his shadow. I became tired of being second best and finally began to do something about it but unfortunately, my dad would never see my success.

Suddenly, my cell phone started ringing. It was Tristan.

"Hey bro, what's up?"

"Hey Ian, I was wondering if you wanted to grab a beer and maybe a game of pool. Kendall's meeting up with Averi at the gym tonight and I thought we'd do a guy's night. You up for it?" Tristan asked.

"Sure! I just had dinner with Mom. Where do you want to meet?" I saw my mom smile as she patted me on the arm.

He paused then said, "Let's meet up at the Junction…say thirty minutes?"

"Sounds good, I'm headed out now." I picked up my keys as I wrapped my arm around her for just one more hug.

"Ok, tell her I love her and I'll see you in a few."

As I hung up my phone, I glanced at my mom who was smiling broadly. "What?" I said returning the smile.

She shrugged. "I guess it just makes me happy to see my boys getting along. It's a mother's dream."

Shaking my head, I laughed. "I'm glad we can make you smile."

She placed her hand on my cheek and her expression suddenly turned serious. "Ian, you are my baby boy and you'll always make me smile. I only pray that you'll find that special someone who will do the same for you."

I sighed. "I thought I might've found her, but as usual, I screwed it up." Quickly kissing her on the forehead, I said,

"Well, I gotta go. Tristan sends his love." I quickly opened the door and escaped before she could interrogate me.

I drove to the Junction and saw Tristan's Jeep was already there. As I walked in, I scanned the room and found him at a pool table in the back. He'd already racked up the balls and had two ice cold beers sitting on a nearby table.

"Are you prepared for an ass-whoopin'?" he asked, giving me a big grin as he chalked his cue.

"Pfft, whatever. You obviously have no idea what you're getting into. Care to make a wager, big brother?" I asked, knowing this was going to be a piece of cake. For the past couple of years, I'd been on a tournament pool team, something Tristan didn't know about.

"Okay, you're on. What do you want?" Tristan said preparing to break for stripes or solids.

I thought for a moment, then smiled. "Anything?"

Tristan paused, the tip of the pool cue poised behind the cue ball. "Sure, why not. I feel pretty confident about kicking your ass."

After I proposed the terms of our wager, Tristan frowned for a moment as he considered it, then he nodded slowly with a smile. "I think that's workable." He leaned over the table, I heard the crack of the balls and our game was on.

Chapter 3

Averi

I felt a tap on my arm startling me out of my daydream.
Pulling my ear buds from my ears, I glanced over to see
Kendall standing on the treadmill next to me with a big
goofy grin on her face. "You should've seen your face,"
she laughed. "You were in another world, weren't you?
Daydreaming about a certain firefighter, perhaps?"

I hit the pause button, wrinkled my nose and shook my
head. "No, I wasn't thinking about Alex," I pouted. "I've
got more serious things to think about right now."

Her eyes grew wide. "What's up? Now you've got me
worried. Let's walk while we talk." She started her
treadmill. I resumed mine, and we got into a steady walking
rhythm.

I began to tell her about the news my parents dropped on
me. "They are so excited, Kendall. I don't want them to be
worried about me but the housing market sucks for the

financially challenged…and in case you're wondering…that would be me."

She nodded thoughtfully. "I totally understand about not wanting to worry or upset them. I remember them talking about their dream of moving to the mountains when I stayed over at your place."

I felt tears spring into my eyes, and I grabbed my workout towel pretending to dab my sweat but instead I dried my eyes without her noticing. "Yeah, as far back as I can remember, Daddy has talked about going back to the mountains where he grew up."

Kendall sped up her treadmill to a jog, and I did the same. I was puffing a little now so I backed the speed back down a little. "I want them to be happy but now I'm freaking out about a place to live."

I heard a beep and looked over to see Kendall had stopped her machine. "Oh gosh, I didn't think about that. You can't stay there?" When I shook my head no, she thought for a moment then said, "Averi, I may have the perfect solution. How'd you like to live in my apartment? Since Tristan and I are living at the house, I'd been thinking of using it as a weekly rental but if you need a place to live, you're more than welcome to stay there!"

My mouth dropped open. "Are you serious? Oh God, Kendall! This would totally save my life!"

She looked at me with surprise. "Of course I'm serious! Why would I even joke about that? You'd also be close to work *and* you could keep an eye on my store for me, as well."

A wave of relief flooded over me. "This is so amazing. I don't know what to say."

She laughed. "How about, 'sure, I'd love to live there' and 'Kendall, you are the bestest ever!' We can start with those."

I stepped off my treadmill and pulled her into a big hug. "I love you, Kendall!" I squealed. A flush came over Kendall's face, and I suddenly realized the gym had gotten really quiet. I looked around and saw we were now the focus of every man in the gym. "Get your minds out of the gutter! Nothing to see here!" I said shaking my head. They went back to their workouts, obviously disappointed we weren't going to provide some hot girl on girl action.

"Come on, let's get out of here," Kendall said stepping off the treadmill. "I'll buy you a beer."

"The perfect post-workout beverage? Sounds good!" I said as we walked into the locker room. I grabbed my bag and began to change from my workout clothes back into my jeans and halter top.

As she changed in the room next to me, she laughed. "Yeah, we'll get lite beer."

Once we'd both changed, we headed out the door to our cars. "Where are we going?" I asked climbing into my Jeep.

She thought for a moment. "Um, we're near The Junction…we could go there, if you want. I think it's two dollar Margarita night!"

"Yum! Sounds good! See you there!" Giving her a wave, I drove out of the parking lot.

Within minutes, I pulled up in front of the bar, grabbed my wallet and hopped out. Kendall had parked a couple of spaces down from me, so I waited for her by the door. While I waited, I sent a text to Alex to let him know where I was. He was working, and I wasn't allowed to call him while he was on duty. I just finished my text when Kendall walked up.

As soon as we walked in, we noticed a crowd gathered at the back of the bar near the pool tables. They were obviously enjoying a pool game by the hoots and whistles. We found a couple of spaces at the bar and ordered our drinks. The cheers for the game got louder and naturally, we became curious, so we picked up our glasses and walked back to see what the excitement was all about. Kendall led the way, but suddenly, I found myself running into her as she stopped in her tracks. Puzzled, I glanced over her shoulder and was surprised to see Tristan. Then I saw Ian. Despite the fact they were in a heated game of pool, they simultaneously looked in our direction as if sensing our presence. Ian was looking way too hot in a black t-shirt paired with faded blue jeans. He had his baseball cap turned backwards and instantly an image of Luke Bryan popped in my head. Ian had obviously been working out, and it showed. Boy, did it show! His t-shirt was stretched across his broad shoulders and chiseled chest. He was lining up to make a shot and without taking his icy blue eyes off of mine, he hit the cue ball which rocketed the final ball into the pocket.

Throwing his hands up in the air, he hollered, "Game!" The crowd erupted in a cheer. "That's best two out of three, brother!" he said placing the pool cue back in the rack before holding his hand out to shake Tristan's. "Do we have a deal?" Tristan laughed and nodded as they shook hands. I had no idea what the bet was and I really didn't care. *Really...didn't...care.* I kept saying that to myself as my heart raced and my palms grew sweaty. Who was I kidding? I really missed seeing him! My internal voice had a meltdown. *What? Averi, really? What about Alex? You have a boyfriend! What are you thinking??*

Tristan moved over to stand beside Kendall, and he wrapped his arm around her waist and spun her into a kiss. Feeling his gaze, my eyes flickered over to Ian briefly then went straight to the big screen TV overhead.

"So, baby. What are you girls up to?" Tristan said nuzzling her ear as he threw his arm over her shoulder.

Kendall grinned. "I've got great news!" she said excitedly.

Tristan smiled. "Do I need to buy a round for the bar? Are we pregnant?"

Kendall laughed. "No, not yet. And yes, that would be exciting news but that's not it."

Tristan pouted then shrugged. "Well, we'll keep trying." He waggled his eyebrows and grinned. "So, you've got something exciting to tell me *and* it turns out I have something exciting to tell you, too!"

Kendall smiled. "You go first, then," she said bumping his hip with hers.

He shook his head and laughed. "Oh no, ladies first."

Kendall looked over at me and smiled. "Well, you remember we were talking about the apartment and what to do with it...I've found a tenant."

Tristan's smile faded. "Um, well that's what I was going to tell you...I've found a tenant," he said frowning.

Wait, what? My heart just stopped. This was not good.

Kendall looked up at Tristan, eyes narrowed. "Well, *honey,* I said Averi could rent it."

Tristan's eyes flickered over to mine before he spoke. "*Baby,* I promised it to Ian."

Following a period of uncomfortable silence I spoke. I couldn't help it. I blurted out, "Kendall promised it to me this afternoon! My parents are moving and I have no place to go!" I felt bad because Tristan and Kendall both looked miserable and at a loss of what to do.

Ian cleared his throat and said, "Tristan lost a bet with me and the prize was the apartment. He lost fair and square."

My head was spinning, and I knew that it wasn't from the drink I'd guzzled. I'd just opened my mouth to speak when I heard him sigh and say, "Look, Averi can have the apartment. *I* can be the *bigger* person. *Despite,* Tristan promising it to *me* because I *really* need a place to stay so I can give you guys some privacy." With every word he emphasized, it made me more and more angry.

I bristled at the insinuation that he was going to be self-sacrificing and the bigger person. My face flushed hot and through gritted teeth I said, "I am *not* going to let you be all noble and stuff." Kendall and Tristan stood silently watching our standoff with obvious discomfort. I glanced at Ian and saw the trace of a smile. Before I could stop myself I said, "Obviously, I wouldn't want to upset either one of you. I'd be willing to share the apartment with him since we're both desperate to find a place…temporarily, of course." I unclenched my teeth and gave them my biggest smile.

Kendall's mouth dropped open and Tristan broke into a big grin. "How's that sound to you, little brother?" He asked slapping Ian on the shoulder.

Ian actually looked stunned as he appeared to be thinking it over. I'd called his bluff and fully expected him to back out. I almost fell over when I heard him say, "Okay, sounds good to me!"

Tristan smiled. "Well, I guess it's settled then. You'll share the apartment until one of you makes other arrangements."

Kendall was whispering furiously in Tristan's ear, but he never stopped grinning. Finally, she said out loud, "There's only one bedroom! What are you going to do about that?"

Ian shrugged. "Averi can have the bedroom, I'll take the futon in the living room. No biggie. I'm always on the go so it'll be just a place to crash." With a deliberate grin directed at me, he said, "We'll just have to share the shower...I mean, bathroom."

Suddenly, it hit me. I'd just agreed to share an apartment with the one man I'd been trying so hard to avoid. And what about Alex? How was I going to explain living with Ian to him? My hands became clammy as the reality of the situation set in. Kendall looked at me with concern. "Averi? You don't look so good. Are you okay?"

I swallowed hard and nodded. "Yeah, sure."

Ian was studying me, and it made me uncomfortable. "You having a change of heart, Little Bit? Want to back out?" He asked, raising his eyebrow.

I took a deep, cleansing breath then shook my head. "Nope, let's do this!"

Chapter 4

Ian

I couldn't believe my ears. Averi was actually agreeing to living with me! I had the irresistible urge to shout but instead tried to play it cool. I could definitely tell this had her rattled, but being a stubborn ass, I wasn't about to let her back out. Plus, I was going to enjoy the hell out of it!

"So, when do *we* move in?" I asked Kendall. Averi winced at the 'we'.

Kendall sighed, shook her head then shrugged. "You can move in whenever you'd like. There's still some furniture in the apartment." She pulled a set of keys from her pocket and removed two of them, handing one to me and one to Averi.

I pocketed the key and as I slapped Tristan on the back, I said, "Well, I think I'll go pack and get out of your hair...and your house."

I was pushed out of the way as Averi went flying by. "Um, I think that's a great idea," she said over her shoulder. "I'll probably beat you there so feel free to let yourself in." She turned and ran out the door.

As I turned to follow her, I found Kendall standing in my way. She was almost as tall as I was and she met me eye to eye. "Ian, what in the hell are you up to?" She asked with a frown.

I held up my hands in defense. "Hey Sis, I'm not up to anything. You guys need your space, I need a place to stay…and Tristan sucks at pool. End of story."

She stared me down, no doubt expecting me to crack and confess some devious intentions, but I just shrugged and smiled.

Tristan wrapped his arm around her again and kissed her cheek. "Wouldn't it be nice to have the house to ourselves, baby?" He started nuzzling her neck and I could see her expression softening.

She turned to look into Tristan's eyes. "Yes, it would…but only if Ian promises he'll be nice." She turned to me. "Ian, seriously. Please don't do this if you just want to mess with her head."

I placed my hand over my heart as if wounded. "Kendall, I swear that's the last thing I would ever do. Plus, we both obviously need somewhere to live and I don't want Averi to end up living in some bus stop or behind a dumpster like a bag lady."

She looked at me closely, then laughed. "Okay, I believe you…but I'll be keeping an eye on you…and you'd better behave."

I kissed her cheek then left her in my brother's capable hands and made my way back to the house to pack. When I got to the house, I wasted no time. I threw some clothes into a couple of duffel bags, strapped my surfboard into the bed of my truck and headed to the apartment. I saw Averi's Jeep parked in the lot and just caught a glimpse of her rapidly rounding the corner of the building as I grabbed my bags. I laughed to myself thinking of how many laws she'd broken to get to her parents' house and back that quickly. As I made my way onto the boardwalk, I could see her balancing a box on her knee as she fumbled with the door lock. She glanced over and when she saw me she frantically jiggled the key, and the box teetered threatening to spill its contents. As she lost her hold, I grabbed for it but missed. The box landed on its side and out tumbled a tangled cluster of lacy thongs, matching bras and other assorted items that apparently stayed in her sock drawer.

My eyes grew wide as I studied the sexy goodies and when I looked up, I saw her face was flushed with embarrassment.

Pretending it was the kind of thing you see every day, I scooped everything into the box, hefted it under my arm and gestured for her to open the door. Taking a deep breath, she unlocked it and propped it open for me. I set her box down and quickly retrieved my bags. By the time I came back in, the box was gone, and she was headed back out for more of her things. I climbed the stairs to the apartment and threw my bags onto the futon. Kendall's apartment wasn't huge, but it was more than enough room for the two of us. It consisted of a bedroom, a full bathroom, a good sized kitchen and a living room. Grabbing one of my duffels, I started to the bathroom to unload my man products. I could hear Averi coming in and out and stopped myself from offering to help her knowing in her present mood, she'd bite my head off. Being a gentleman, I decided to ask her which side of the vanity she wanted, but I stopped short when I heard her talking quietly on her cell phone when I opened the door.

"Alex, there's absolutely nothing going on with Ian." I pulled the door almost shut but left it cracked open just enough to hear her end of the conversation. I saw her quickly glance over to the door. "Well, I guess we *could* have moved in together but I think that implies we're a lot more serious than we are. I'm not ready for that yet." She paused. "No, I don't see him like that, he's just a roommate. This is purely for convenience." *So, Alex was upset. Points for me!* "You are more than welcome to come over any time and see exactly what's going on…nothing!"

I couldn't resist the impulse, so I opened the door and said very loudly, "Averi, which side of the vanity do you want me to put my stuff on, since we're sharing?"

She hit the mute button. "I really don't care!" she hissed. "You pick."

She unmuted the call and even without speaker phone, I could hear Alex's voice very plainly say, "I don't like this at all!" For privacy, she walked into the bedroom and shut her door effectively preventing me from eavesdropping any further. I removed my things from my bag and placed them on the widest part of the vanity. Tossing the rest of my stuff under the sink, I was opening the door to come out when I almost ran right into her. She looked around me to see what I'd been up to.

"So, you chose the best side, huh?" She asked as she gestured to my arrangement.

"You gave up dibs. That's just the way I roll. Next time you'll think before you leave the decision up to me." I stepped around her and walked into the living room which I realized was now my bedroom. I kicked off my shoes, grabbed the remote and laid down on the futon. "So, what time's dinner?" I asked scrolling through the channels.

"Dinner? Are you nuts? Do you expect me to wait on you?" She stomped over, grabbed the remote from my hand and shut it off. "I think it's time to lay down some ground rules."

I sat up and politely folded my hands. "Okay, then I think we *each* should get to set some rules…since we're sharing the place equally."

She narrowed her eyes. "Well, I guess that's only fair. I'll go first."

I shrugged. "Sounds good. Hit me with the first one."

She held up one finger. "Rule number one is we each have to cook for ourselves."

I nodded in agreement. "Okay, but what if one of us *wants* to cook for both of us?" I asked.

She thought for a moment. "Well, then I guess that would be okay but I don't see that happening. We'll just see how that goes. Okay, now you get to make a rule."

I thought for a moment. "Rule two. If either of us has a date over, the other has to find somewhere else to hang out until said date is over."

Averi frowned. "I don't think I like that. With your reputation, I'll never get to sleep in my own bed!"

My eyes grew wide. "Damn. That's harsh." I sat back on the couch clutching my chest. "That was a shot to the heart."

Placing one hand on her hip, she rolled her eyes. "Ian, you know it's true. Please respect me and don't bring your beach bunnies here. I promise that if I ever want to spend the night with Alex, we'll find somewhere else to go."

Just the mention of Alex's name made me clench my fists but the 'if' helped me keep my cool. Guess ole' Alex wasn't an overnighter yet. Then I realized what she'd said. "Beach bunnies? What in the hell are beach bunnies?"

She laughed. "Beach bunnies would be the hordes of bikini clad bimbos that are constantly hovering around you twenty-four hours a day. I really don't see how you have time to work, eat or sleep with all you have to keep up with."

I pouted my lips. "Averi, I can't turn off the mojo. All the ladies seem to love me...*except* you. I still don't know what I did to make you hate me so much but hopefully after living with me for a while, you'll see a different Ian."

Her face clouded over at the word hate. "I don't *hate* you." Then she shrugged. "We'll see how this goes. Anyway, you will do your own laundry, clean your side of the apartment and I'll do mine. I'm not going to be your maid and cook."

I nodded and stood to tower over her. "Got it. Well, I'm going to hit the beach for a while and let you unpack your toy box..."

Her head whipped around. "What did you say?"

"I'm going to hit the beach for a while?" I asked playing coy.

"No, not that part," she said poking me in the chest. Her cheeks were red with embarrassment.

I broke into a huge smile. "OH, you mean the part about the toy box. Well, hey I'm not gonna judge. If it makes you happy…" With an exaggerated wink I said, "Go play and I'll catch you later, Little Bit." I left her standing there with her mouth hanging open to dig around in my bag for my board shorts. I hit the bathroom for a quick change and headed out the door never once looking back at her.

The sun was setting as I finished jogging a few miles on the beach then I wandered back up to the apartment. This was a sweet setup. I really liked how close it was to the beach and was *very* thankful that I had a pretty good game of pool. Tristan bet the apartment and lost and the part of the bet that Kendall and Averi didn't know was it was rent-free. My brother balked at that stipulation at first but then agreed to cover the rent so that Kendall would still get a little money for it. My intention with the bet was to try to save enough money to get my own place eventually but having Averi as a roommate only sweetened the deal. I strolled up the stairs and saw a towel on the doorknob. Puzzled, I pulled it off, opened the door and found Averi and Alex watching a movie on the couch. "Hey Averi, did you know there was a towel on the doorknob?" I asked as I walked through to the kitchen. I was rummaging in the fridge to see what groceries she'd brought when she came up behind me.

"Yes, I did, since I *put* it there!" She whispered with irritation.

I whispered back. "Was that some kind of signal?" Okay, so my whisper wasn't really a whisper.

She glanced back to see if Alex was listening but he appeared to be watching the movie. "Yes, I stuck it there as a signal for you to give me some space for a while. Can't you find somewhere to hang out?"

"My first night here and you're throwing me out already?" She glared at me, so I held up my hands in surrender. "Okay, I gotcha. I just need to hop in the shower first and then I'll go grab some dinner in town."

She sighed. "Good. I don't want Alex to be madder than he already is."

I walked back through the living room and waved at Alex as I passed by. "Hey man! How's it going?" I said giving him a nod. He briefly glanced my way then turned back to the movie. Guess he wasn't feeling sociable. In the bathroom, I was already undressed and was just about to get in the shower when I remembered I'd left all of my clothes in the living room. I quickly wrapped a towel around my waist and strolled out. "Hey, Averi. Can you grab my duffel for me? I need my clothes."

The reaction I got from both of them was exactly the one I wanted. Averi, who'd been about to take a drink, ended up choking on it then sat with her mouth hanging open. Alex, on the other hand, was glaring at me looking pretty ticked off. Averi jumped up and grabbed my bag tossing it at me angrily, and as she did, I let go of the towel. Thankfully, the bag now in my hands covered my nakedness, and I saw her face flush red as she realized what she'd done. I don't know what possessed me, but I nonchalantly turned and walked back into the bathroom leaving them a perfect view of my very bare backside.

As I shut the door, I could hear their voices get louder and louder, and I knew I'd pushed Alex's buttons. A few minutes later, I heard the slam of the apartment door, and I quickly finished dressing. Cautiously, I opened the bathroom door and could see Averi in her bedroom sprawled on her bed, obviously crying. I walked up to the door and gently knocked. "Hey, I hope I didn't do anything to cause you guys to fight. I didn't mean to, if I did." The fact that I did instigate things was really for her own good.

She sniffled and wiped her eyes as she sat up. "No, it wasn't all about you. You *did* have something to do with it when you paraded around as naked as the day you were born, but he's mad about our whole roommate situation. It'll be okay. He'll get used to it." She covered her face with her hands, and I heard her murmur, "He has to."

After an awkward silence, I said, "Well, since I'm hungry and you're alone…why don't I order some pizza for dinner? My treat."

Slowly uncovering her face, she gave me a half smile. "I am kinda hungry. Okay, but don't let this become a habit." I ordered the pizza and when it arrived, I called her to come to eat. She'd washed her face and had her hair piled up in a messy bun. She looked so sexy I almost dropped my beer. Wearing a cropped tank and shorts she made herself comfortable sitting cross-legged on the floor. We ate in silence, the sound of the television in the background. I tried not to be obvious, but I was totally mesmerized by her natural beauty and wanted to kick myself for all the years I'd been so blind to what was right in front of me. None of the women I'd dated could even compare and sitting here with her, I realized I couldn't even remember any of them with any clarity. The odds of getting her to give me a chance was slim, but I knew I had to keep trying because she was most certainly worth it. Something on the TV caught her attention, and she laughed. "I love this movie!"

Glancing over, I saw it was 'Pitch Perfect'. "Oh yeah, I've seen this. It's pretty good."

Brows raised and mouth open, she stared at me. "Pretty good? Aca-scuse me? This is like the most amazing movie ever!"

I laughed. "Well, I don't know. I prefer the old action movies like 'Top Gun'. Too many good quotes from that one to pick a favorite."

Shrugging, she smiled. "I feel the need…the need for speed. I've seen that one a lot too. That's probably my daddy's favorite movie."

"So, how many times have you watched this?" I asked laughing.

"Probably twenty or so. I've got the DVD. It has bonus scenes!" She picked up the DVD case and tossed it to me.

As the finale came on, she quietly sang along with the music. "You're welcome to sing for me," I said turning the volume down with the remote, so I could hear her better.

She glanced over her shoulder. "Uh, no. You'll never hear me sing…ever. It's not fit for human ears. My best singing is in my Jeep at 60 mph with the top down."

I chuckled. "As Mark Twain said, 'Sing like no one's listening, love like you've never been hurt, dance like nobody's watching, and live like its heaven on earth.'"

She turned to face me. "You know Mark Twain?" Then she laughed and shook her head. "Did they teach you that in lifeguard school? Ian, you never cease to amaze me."

"Averi, despite what you think of me, I actually have a brain and do try to use it sometimes. I have many sides, you've just seen my bad ones."

"Yeah, you're right." She nodded slowly then stood abruptly. "Well, I guess I'll turn in. Thanks for dinner," she said as she began to gather up our plates.

"I'll get those," I said, my hand brushing hers, and I took them from her. Time stood still for a moment until finally I broke the silence. "Averi, you get some sleep. I'll see you tomorrow."

She looked up at me, hesitated as if she wanted to say something, but instead she turned and walked into her room where she gently shut the door.

Chapter 5

Averi

Shutting the door behind me, I leaned against it as I let out a sigh. I'd anticipated this arrangement was going to be difficult, but this was insane. Ian was gorgeous, funny, thoughtful, but was still a major pain in my ass. And I still loved him. I threw myself on the bed and closing my eyes, I pictured Alex. He was tall, muscular and most definitely handsome, but he didn't make my heart race like Ian did. On top of his irresistible physical charms, he was actually normal when he wasn't putting on a show for the ladies. Just the thought of him kissing me at the wedding made my heart race. I'd waited for that to happen for so long, and it was more incredible than I'd ever dreamed. For months, I'd shut my feelings off for him but with that one kiss, he'd ripped them wide open again. A text on my phone interrupted my thoughts, and I grabbed it to see who it was. It was Alex.

Hey, I'm sorry. I just don't know if I can handle this.

My heart fell. Alex deserved a chance, and I knew this was going to end if I didn't let this stupid infatuation with Ian go.

With a deep breath, I responded.

I'll see what I can do to make him move out. It has to be his decision since he technically has the right to be here.

I could see he was typing his response.

I'll give you some time because I really do care. Goodnight.

I lay there, tears seeping from my eyes. This wasn't going to be easy, but somehow, I had to make Ian so miserable, he'd want to leave. I tossed my phone onto the dresser, climbed under the covers and fell into a fitful sleep.

The next morning, I crawled from my bed, grabbed my things to shower and headed to the bathroom. As I passed the fridge, I noticed that Ian had posted a calendar and today's date showed that he had an important meeting at nine. I glanced at the clock and saw it was a little before eight, and he was still snoring on the futon. Alex's text came to mind. To make him happy, I just had to sabotage our roommate agreement, so I crept across the room, found his phone and moved his alarm ahead thirty minutes. I dashed into the bathroom, plugged in my hair dryer and straightener then jumped in the shower. I took a long, hot shower intending to use all of the hot water. When I heard the alarm go off and noises in the living room, I could just picture his expression when he realized he was most definitely going to be late.

"Averi? Are you almost finished in there?" He asked as he gently knocked on the door.

 "Um, no…I just got in the shower," I yelled over the sounds of the shower.

There no response, then I heard, "Ah, screw it!"

The door opened, and I could see through the shower curtain that Ian had walked right in. Immediately, I grabbed the towel hanging over the shower rod to cover myself. "HEY! Get out! I'm showering here!"

He was turned toward the mirror, and I saw him shrug. "I can take it if you can. I've got to shave and get dressed so it looks like we're gonna be sharing this morning."

Stunned, I shut off the water which had now thoroughly soaked my towel and stood there with my mouth open. "Are you serious? I need my privacy."

He turned and whipped open the curtain making me clutch the towel tightly around me. "Privacy? You have a bedroom. Let's talk about *my* bed being in the middle of the apartment. I think you've got more than enough privacy, darlin'."

I pouted my lips. "Well, then if you don't like it, leave!" I huffed.

Suddenly, his expression softened and he broke into a smile. "Is that what you're trying to do? Make me mad enough to leave? Good luck, sweetheart. I'm here to stay."

Pulling the curtain closed, he then turned back to the sink, wiping the moisture from the mirror in a tiny circle. After quickly shaving, he brushed his teeth and ran his fingers through his hair. I stood stupefied. He glanced over to where I was still standing dripping wet in the shower and said, "You're lucky I took a shower last night. If I hadn't, I'd have hopped right in there with you." With a huge cheesy smile, he took one last look in the mirror and left, closing the door behind him. It took a moment for me to digest fully what had just happened. This was more than I could process, and I realized my legs were like jelly. I climbed from the shower and sat down on the edge of the tub. I heard the front door shut and knew he was gone.

Grabbing a fresh towel, I dried off then slipped on my clothes. The unmistakable scent of his cologne still lingered in the room, so I closed my eyes and breathed it in. Watching him doing his morning routine had been so intimate and only made me wish we were more than roommates. I closed my eyes and fantasized. In the place of the awkwardly tense encounter we'd just had, I pictured myself showering, the steam like a shroud surrounding me. After a soft knock, I hear the bathroom door open and gently close. Holding my breath with anticipation, I only hear the rushing of the water. As the curtain is slowly being pulled back, my heart begins to pound. I slowly turn to see Ian's crystal blue eyes locked onto mine. With a sexy smile, he climbs into the shower with me, his eyes hungrily taking in the sight of the warm water cascading down my body. As if hypnotized, my eyes drift down to his chiseled chest, his ripped abs. Pulling me to him, he pauses, licks his lips then presses his lips to mine, our wet, naked bodies pressing against each other...

"AVERI?" I almost fell on the floor as I heard Kendall call out as she knocked at the front door. "You ready for your coffee?"

"Be down in a minute!" I croaked, my voice all weird sounding from my daydream.

"You got a cold or something?" she asked with concern. "Do you want me to make some tea instead of coffee this morning?"

I cleared my throat then yelled back, "No, just got a frog this morning. Coffee's fine. Meet you downstairs in five minutes." She headed back down the stairs, and I turned to my mirror. "Averi, you are such a loser," I said to my flushed reflection. "He's obviously playing games with you. Woman, you need to build a bridge and get over it!" I scolded the pitiful image staring back at me. Skipping the blow dryer, I roughly pulled my damp hair up into a ponytail, grabbed my keys and headed down to start my day.

After Kendall and I had our morning coffee, I made my way to the store. Kendall studied me for a few minutes when I first walked in, and I could sense she wanted to ask me if I was okay. Thank goodness for George. George, a widower in his eighties, was a fixture in the coffee shop. After encouraging him for months, he informed us he finally had gone online to a dating website and was now dating a seventy-something widow. We grilled him for details while I ate my muffin and drank my coffee and he happily obliged. Instead of lingering, he drank his coffee quickly and explained he was meeting his new lady friend for a walk on the beach. With a wave, he was gone. Before Kendall could turn her attention back to me, I dashed out shouting, "Would you look at the time? See ya!" After applying henna to several customers, I decided to refresh the ones on the back of my hands that had faded before I cleaned up for the day. I was totally engrossed with my work when I heard the doorbell ring, and two women walked in.

"Sharon, I don't know what I'm going to do. I can't keep my baby."

The other woman placed her hand on her shoulder. "Do you think someone would take him? He's absolutely adorable. Did you ask your parents if they'd help you out?"

She shook her head no. "They said they've raised all they're going to and that I got into this and I'll have to figure my way out."

They both stopped talking when they saw me looking at them from behind the counter. "Something I can do for you ladies?" I asked as I cleaned up my henna tools.

Sharon smiled. "Yes, we'd like to get matching henna tattoos, please."

They spent a few minutes picking out the one they wanted, and I began to apply the stain. When I was halfway through the first one, they struck up their conversation again. "I think I'll just put him up for adoption. They're cute when they're little but when they grow up, that's another story. It gets harder to find people who want to take them."

I was confused. Were they talking about her kid? Sharon shook her head. "Becca, don't do that. I'm sure you could find someone willing to give him a home."

Finally, I had to speak up. "Excuse me. Are you talking about giving up your kid for adoption? You may not want my opinion but I'm gonna give it. I don't know your situation but that's a dumb move. You're his mother, you should want to keep him."

They both stared at me with their mouths open, then they started laughing. Becca spoke. "A baby? No, we're talking about my puppy, Tiny. I totally fell in love with him but now have to find him a home. I've tried to find someone to take him but may end up leaving him at the shelter."

A dog? Going to the shelter? "What kind of dog is he? I might be interested," I asked impulsively.

Becca smiled. "Well, I could lie and tell you a Chihuahua but in fact, he's a four week old Great Dane and he weighs about five pounds. My boyfriend and I are living together and when I brought him home, he flipped out. He convinced me that even though he was totally precious right now, he is going to be a huge dog when he's grown. He said it was either him or the dog so I had to choose my man. I do want to find him a good home though. He's too sweet to drop off at the shelter or throw out on the street."

At the mention of her boyfriend's ultimatum, an idea popped in my head. If Kendall would let me have him, he just might be the perfect solution for my dilemma with Ian. What better persuasion to move than a huge dog slobbering all over his things. I knew Kendall was a push-over for pet rescues so I felt pretty confident this could work out.

"Hey, I might have a solution for you. Let me call my friend." I grabbed my cell and dialed Kendall.

"Hey, what's up?" She asked sounding rushed.

"You busy? I need to ask you a question."

She laughed. "Of course, I'm always busy, but never too busy for you."

"Well, I wanted to know if you would let me have a puppy in the apartment. His owner has to find a home for him soon or she'll have to leave him at the shelter." My voice dropped to a whisper, "You *know* what happens if they don't get adopted." I was deliberately vague about exactly what *kind* of puppy.

"Um, well, sure. You know I don't mind. Ian likes dogs so it shouldn't bother him. Just keep him in your room if it does. You guys can work it out, I'm sure. I've got to run but it sounds okay to me."

"Okay, thanks so much!" I hung up the phone and smiled. "Looks like he has a home."

I got her number and address and told her I'd be over as soon as I closed. I could barely contain my excitement as I rushed over and the moment he came bounding out of his crate, I fell in love. He stopped when he saw me, then came slowly forward, and I immediately noticed his eyes. One was pale ice blue and the other was a deep dark blue. He had a pink nose and lips and it made him look as if he were smiling at me. I picked him up and he yawned in my face, and I breathed in his puppy breath and smiled. "Oh, he's precious!" I gushed.

Becca gave me his carrier, toys and collar and when I tried to pay her, she waved it away. "You don't owe me a thing. I'm just happy that he'll have a good home."

With my squirming bundle in my arms, I climbed into the Jeep and put him safely in the carrier. He whined a little but soon fell asleep as we drove down the road. I looked for Ian's truck in the parking lot but thankfully didn't see it. I scooped up my new baby with his things and carried him up to the apartment. I put his things in my room and decided I'd better keep him out of sight at first. He was so full of energy after his nap and bounded around my room for about five minutes before he ran out of steam. He fell asleep with his head on one of my fuzzy slippers. I grabbed my laptop and googled Great Danes to get an idea of what I'd gotten myself into. I found out he was what they refer to as a Harlequin due to his coloring. I also discovered that he could weigh up to 150 pounds by the time he was full grown! I looked down at the fat-bellied puppy by my feet then back at the picture of the adult Dane on my screen. It was incredible that he would become that big and for a moment, I doubted my decision to take him, but then I remembered the fate of so many pets left at a shelter, and I brushed it aside. He was mine, and he was here to stay.

Chapter 6

Ian

I dragged myself up the stairs to the apartment feeling like I'd been run over by a truck. It felt like the longest day in history. After arriving late for my meeting, I'd spent the entire day following my boss around to the other meetings she had. A dinner meeting with the CEO finished out the day then I went back to the office to catch up on emails and voicemails so I wouldn't be swamped and get even further behind the next day. I checked the doorknob and seeing no 'signal', I unlocked the door to find the lights off and the apartment quiet. After a quick shower, I threw myself on the futon and within minutes was soon fast asleep.

Whimpering. I could swear I heard whimpering. I cracked my eyes open and could just make out the outline of Averi creeping across the room.

"You okay?" I said propping myself on my elbows.

She jumped and clutched her heart. "Oh my God! You scared the crap out of me!"

I laughed. "Sorry, your crying woke me up." I reached up and turned on the table lamp, and she squinted her eyes against the sudden brightness.

"Crying? What are you talking about?" She asked scrunching up her nose.

Suddenly, I heard a tiny squeak and then a whine. "That…that's what I'm talking about." It was then I noticed the tiny bundle tucked under her arm. "Is that a puppy?"

She shrugged, avoiding eye contact. "Kinda?"

I narrowed my eyes. "How is that 'kinda' a puppy? Is it yours?"

She sighed. "Well, yes, he's mine. He's here because his owner was only hours from dumping him at a shelter, or worse…out on the street. I just had to save him."

I sat up and motioned to her. "Let me see what you've got." She walked over then perched on the edge of the futon and I immediately caught the fragrance of coconut. Having Averi sitting so close to me was intoxicating. Her hair was loose and hanging over her shoulder concealing the squirming pup in her arms. I brushed back her hair to reveal two blue eyes and a pink nose. "Is he a Dalmatian?" I asked trying to figure him out.

She hesitated then shrugged again. "Um, not sure. They really didn't know. He's four weeks old and weighs five pounds."

He worked his way out of her arms and was climbing up the blanket toward me. I picked him up and looked into his eyes. "He's really cute. What's his name?"

"Tiny," she said with a smile. "His name fits him, don't ya think?"

Tiny's pink tongue lapped out to catch me right on the end of my nose. "Yeah, he's definitely tiny. I assume you're going to be responsible for him. I don't mind dogs but I didn't sign up for one, just an apartment. Are we going to need to make a new roommate rule?"

"No, we don't need to amend the roommate agreement. We were just on our way out." She scooped him back up into her arms. "Sorry we woke you. I'll try to be quieter next time." I detected a trace of sarcasm. She tucked her hair behind her ear and again the fragrance of coconut wafted by my nose. Thoughts of burying my face in her hair and running my hands through its silkiness flashed through my mind. "Um, you okay? You kinda glazed over for a minute."

I blinked and shook my head to clear it. "Oh…sure. I had a long day and I'm just exhausted. I also wanted to apologize for this morning. I shouldn't have barged in on you. That was disrespectful and I'm sorry."

She nodded then gave me a half smile. "It's okay. I was being a bathroom hog. I need to learn to share." Cradling Tiny in her arms, she stood to leave. "Again, I'm sorry we woke you," she said softly. "Goodnight."

I lay back down then cradled my head in my hands to watch her go out the door. Once she'd closed it, I got up, threw on some shorts and quietly followed her outside to make sure she was safe. I kept in the shadows and watched her place Tiny on a patch of grass. He snuffled around for a moment then I heard her say, "Good boy!" After a few more minutes, she scooped him up, so I dashed back up the stairs into the apartment and back into my bed. Quietly, she opened the door and crept in, shushing Tiny as he whimpered and struggled to lick her face. She crossed the room to hers and silently shut the door behind her.

It was still dark when I woke to the sound of scratching coming from behind her door. Puzzled, I got up and eased her door open. She was sprawled across the bed, her raven hair cascading over her pillow, her lips slightly open, her eyes tightly shut. Tiny's whimper got my attention. He was obviously in need of a potty break, so I picked him up and took him downstairs. After he'd finished his business, instead of putting him back with Averi, I tucked him in bed with me. He curled into my body, sighed, and we were soon fast asleep again.

"Tiny!" Averi said softly. "Where are you?" She came running out of her room and stopped in her tracks. Seeing Tiny tucked in the crook of my arm, she asked, "How did he get in here?"

Careful not to wake him, I whispered, "He needed Uncle Ian to take him out so I did. We didn't want to wake you."

She dropped into the easy chair next to the futon then tucked her feet under her. "Thank you," she said with a smile. "I must've been dead asleep."

I nodded. "Yeah, the snoring and drooling were a good sign that you were out."

Her face flushed red. "Drooling? Snoring? I don't think so!" She scoffed. "I've never been told I do either of those things."

I cocked my eyebrow. "Not even by lover boy Alex?"

Shaking her head, she said, "Not that it's any of your business but we've never spent the entire night together. He usually has to go home to rest for his strange hours at work."

This was good news for me and told me everything I needed to know. I still had a chance. "So, let me ask you something," I said shifting Tiny so his nails weren't digging in my side. "Why didn't you think of sharing an apartment with him? You've been dating for a while now."

Her eyes avoided mine. "Well, I'm trying not to rush into anything. Dating is one thing but being in a committed relationship is something I'm not ready for. At least not yet."

Our voices had woken Tiny, and he stirred in my arms, then opened his eyes. When he saw Averi, he yawned then I swear he smiled. He crawled down the blanket toward her, his tail wagging. She got up and came over to the futon, so I patted the space beside me. "Sit. I promise, I won't bite."

She laughed as she sat on the edge, her hand absently scratching Tiny behind his ear. He rolled over onto his back, and his legs began to kick when she scratched his good spot. We sat like that for a while, watching Tiny bite the air, his paws, our fingers and even my blanket. It felt so good, so natural. I wanted every morning to be this way, waking up together.

My phone vibrated and as I checked the number, I saw Averi quickly glance at it as well. It was Andrea, a girl I'd dated a couple of times before but instead of answering, I quickly rejected the call. Averi's brows raised. "Ian, you don't have to ignore your women. I can give you some privacy." Before I could speak, she scooped Tiny into her arms and walked into her bedroom, firmly shutting the door. Crap! It always seemed as if my past wanted to keep biting me in the ass.

When I arrived at work, I got the news that I was going to be leaving with Tristan on a business trip to California the next day and would be gone for two weeks. Ignoring my protests, Tristan made it clear that it was good for my career. Reluctantly, I agreed but all I could think of was losing ground to Alex.

That night, as I climbed the stairs to the apartment, I could hear voices.

"Why did you get a damn dog? I don't like dogs!" Alex was shouting.

There was a sniffle then I heard Averi say, "But he needed a home. They were going to put him to sleep!"

He huffed, "Well, you can lock him up when I come over. I don't want him slobbering all over my clothes."

She pleaded, "But he's only a puppy, he'll cry if I lock him up."

There was a moment of silence then I heard him say, "Do it or I'm not coming back."

I quietly backed down a couple of steps then noisily clomped my way up to the door making sure they'd heard me. The voices abruptly silenced. I rattled the doorknob as I put my key in and when I opened the door, Alex was sitting on my futon, and Averi was coming from her room shutting the door behind her. Tiny was whimpering and scratching at the door, and it made me furious. Alex had his eyes glued to the television so catching Averi's eyes, I gave her a warm smile which she returned.

"Where's my little man?" I asked, deliberately looking around the room and into the kitchen.

She sighed. "He's in the bedroom for a little while."

I narrowed my eyes. "Well, I was looking forward to seeing him." I continued, "I'm going to be going out of town for a couple of weeks and I need my puppy fix."

At the mention of my going away, her smile faded. "You're leaving? When?"

I nodded as I grabbed some bread and cold cuts to make a sandwich. "Yeah, Tristan and I are going to L.A. for business." I made sure to speak loud enough for Alex to hear me. "We've got important meetings and we're flying out in the morning."

Averi bit her lower lip then sighed. "Well, you have a nice trip and I guess I'll see you when you get back." She walked over to the futon where she plopped down next to Alex. He gave me a smug look of satisfaction, but it quickly faded as I gathered up my sandwich and dropped right down on the futon beside him.

"Hope you don't mind, but you're sitting on my bed. I don't mind Averi on it, for obvious reasons, but you're not my type." Taking a big bite, I leaned back and began happily munching away.

Within a couple of minutes, Alex said in a low voice into her ear, "I've got to go. It's getting crowded in this apartment. I'll talk to you tomorrow." Averi walked him to the door. As he reached it, he turned back to me and with one final glare, he growled to Averi, "Keep your door locked. I don't trust him."

I threw up my hands and laughed. "Dude, I'm the one who needs a locking door! I can't keep her away from me!"

The door slammed then he clumped down the stairs. Shaking her head, Averi asked, "Why do you insist on doing that? It's like you enjoy it or something." She opened the door and followed him out. As soon as they were both gone, I opened Averi's bedroom door and picked up Tiny, who was now blissfully gnawing on a flip flop. I put him on my futon and pulled out one of the chew toys I got him on my way home. When Averi came back into the apartment, she said, "So, are you happy now? Are you *trying* to ruin my love life?"

I smirked and shook my head. "Little Bit, if that's your idea of a love life, you'd be better off alone."

She put her hands on her hips and pouted. "For God's sake, how many times do I have to tell you not to call me Little Bit? It's annoying!"

I shrugged. "Maybe a million? I've always called you that and I like it. Anyway, quit trying to change the subject. Obviously, he isn't into the same things you are. When are you going to wake up?"

She suddenly turned her attention to Tiny, avoiding eye contact *and* the question. "Where did he get a rawhide?"

"Uncle Ian brought it home for him." I reached down and scratched under his chin watching as his back leg paddled the air uncontrollably. "He loves his Uncle Ian…don't you buddy?"

A strange expression crossed Averi's face. She bent down, picked him up and cuddled him under her chin as he squirmed to get to me, his mouth snapping at the air as his tongue flapped sloppily. "Um, thanks. That was nice of you."

I shrugged my shoulders. "Yeah, I even surprise myself sometimes."

She bit her lip, her eyes looking up into mine. "Have a safe trip, Ian. Tiny would be heartbroken if anything happened to you." She turned and as she walked to her room she glanced back at me giving me a sad smile. I broke into a grin as her door closed behind her.

Chapter 7

Averi

Ian had only been gone a week, but I missed him like crazy. It was insane that my feelings for him were growing stronger every day instead of the opposite. Alex had come over a couple of times when he wasn't working but I actually dreaded his visits now because I had to lock Tiny in my bedroom the entire time he was there. And Tiny wasn't so *tiny* anymore. He'd been less than five pounds when I got him and now he was almost ten. He also started chewing on everything he could find, which now included my surviving flip flop, my beautiful designer sunglasses and a pair of my favorite underwear. Kendall came up to see him, and I knew from the 'what the hell' look on her face that she knew he was going to be big. I couldn't keep my secret from her any longer, so I confessed that he was a Great Dane and after a moment of silence, she nodded then said, "I trust you know what you're doing. Just don't let him eat my furniture."

My parents were only days from moving so I took Tiny over to see them, and they fell in love with him right away. They marveled at how much he ate and how big his feet were. I helped them pack some boxes and load them into the PODS container they were using to move. As we packed, it started to hit me that they were really moving away and weren't going to be right around the corner. My dad pulled me aside and tucked some money in my hand. "Here…use this for emergencies but don't tell your mom. She said you need to learn to be independent. It'll be our secret."

A few minutes later, my mom called me to help her pack something in the bathroom and when we were alone, she whispered as she pressed some cash in my hand, "Here's some money in case you need it. Don't tell your dad, he's trying to make you independent. It'll be our secret."

I wanted to laugh out loud and tell them, but then I realized it would only hurt their feelings. I accepted the money and vowed to put it away and give it back to them somehow without their knowing. Ian's part of the rent was making my life easier and helped me pay for Tiny's food, which was already getting expensive.

When moving day finally arrived, I came over to find they'd finished packing and had their car loaded with the essentials they'd need when they got to their new home. Their stuff in the container was going to be taken within the week, and it was crammed full with the rest of their household items.

We did a final walk through on the house to make sure they hadn't forgotten anything, and a flood of memories came rushing over me. I'd grown up in that house and under the layers of paint, there were my crudely drawn crayon pictures of unicorns and rainbows. The notches on the door frame measuring my height were still visible because they didn't want to paint those away. My dad checked his watch and announced they needed to get going. He wanted to 'hit the road' while the traffic was light, so they put the last of their things in the car and turned to say goodbye. I saw tears welling in my mom's eyes, and I felt a huge lump form in my throat. "Sweetie, we're not going that far..." she said, her voice breaking.

My dad put his arm around her and kissed the side of her face. "Averi, you know we love you and will be just a phone call away," he said holding out his other arm to encircle my shoulders. We formed a circle and hugged each other, my mom sobbing on my shoulder. The weird thing was, I couldn't cry. Dry-eyed, I stood there patting my mom on the back, and I felt absolutely awful about it. They were moving away and I wouldn't see them every day, but I couldn't find any tears. My dad finally pulled my mom away to lead her to the car. Once she was safely inside, he turned and gave me one last hug. "We love you, Averi." He climbed into the car, and I saw my mom give me a little wave before hiding behind a Kleenex. They drove away as I stood on the curb waving at them until they were out of sight.

I wandered to the backyard to find Tiny chasing a yellow butterfly. Smiling, I picked him up before he could catch it. As I gazed at his beautiful blue eyes, he playfully licked my nose, exhaling his exquisite puppy breath in my face. Giggling, I gave him a squeeze then said, "Looks like it's just us, little man." I loaded him into my Jeep and drove back to my empty apartment. Once inside, I gave him a bowl of food and curled up on the futon which still had the lingering scent of Ian's aftershave. I was lost in thought when my phone chimed with a text from Alex.

I got called in to work. Won't make it by tonight. Sorry.

I typed a 'K' in response surprisingly relieved that I wouldn't have to hide my puppy for the evening. Tiny had fallen asleep on the floor beside the futon and was snoring happily. I watched him, a smile curling the corner of my mouth. I was still holding my phone when it rang. It was Ian. I hesitated for a moment, my finger poised over the 'reject call' button, but I finally answered. I really wanted to hear his voice.

"Hello?"

"Hey Averi!" he said. "I just called to check in to make sure you're okay."

Puzzled, I asked, "Why would you do that? Why would you think I wasn't okay?"

He paused for a moment. "I dunno, I was just making sure you were locking the door and being extra careful when you take Tiny out."

Indignantly, I huffed, "I'm more than capable of taking care of myself, thank you!"

There was a long pause then he said softly, "I'm sorry if I bothered you."

It suddenly hit me how nasty I'd been. I softened my tone and said, "I'm sorry, Ian. I appreciate you checking in on me. I've really had a crappy day, to be honest."

"You want to talk about it?" he asked. "I have nowhere to be."

Biting my lip, I said, "Well, my parents moved today."

I could hear him rustling around before he spoke, "I'm sorry...that had to be tough. I know you're going to miss them."

Suddenly, I realized how stupid I was being. "Gosh, Ian. Here I am whining about my parents *moving* and you just *lost* your dad. I'm so sorry."

He hesitated then said, "Thanks. Tell ya what, let's talk about something else. How's my little man?"

"Oh, he's doing great! Growing like a weed," I said glancing down at my enormous puppy who'd already doubled in size since Ian left. "You'll hardly recognize him by the time you get back." I dropped my hand over the side of the futon to give his belly a scratch.

He laughed. "Well, I've got a few new goodies for him. I know what you're going to say but I like spoiling him."

I loved hearing him say that. "So," I said softly, "tell me about your work." As I lay there listening to Ian, I realized just how much I missed him. His voice was soothing and combined with his scent on the futon, it made me feel even closer to him. He talked about his work with Tristan, and I closed my eyes imagining him lying next to me, my head resting on his chest as he told me about his day.

We talked for a few more minutes until I couldn't hold back a yawn. "Well, Averi," he said, "I know it's late there so I'm going to let you get to sleep. I'll be back in about a week. In the meantime, if you want to talk, call me anytime. If I don't answer, I'll call you back as soon as I can." Nodding, I held the phone tightly. "You still there?" he asked. I could hear him breathing softly.

"Yes, and thank you for calling, Ian," I said quietly.

"Goodnight, Little Bit," he whispered.

For the first time, it didn't make me angry to hear that. It made me feel good. "Goodnight, Ian."

I picked up Tiny, took him outside for his nightly ritual, being sure to heed Ian's warning by making sure to look around carefully for any sign of danger. I came back into the apartment but instead of going to my bedroom to sleep,

I lay back down on the futon with my puppy sprawled across my chest and fell into a dreamless sleep.

The next morning, Tiny woke me by licking my face. I had to go to work so after feeding him his breakfast, which he quickly inhaled, I put him in his crate to keep him safe while I was gone. My store was right downstairs so I could come back and check on him several times during the day. I gave him a biscuit on my way out and left him munching happily as I shut the door. Kendall looked up as I came into the coffee shop. "Good morning, bestie!" she said as she grabbed a cup to make my usual order. "How's the horse?"

Rolling my eyes, I mumbled hello. I was not coherent until I had my coffee, and she knew the routine. I plopped down at my usual table and within moments, my steaming coffee was placed in front of me. George came in for his morning coffee and Danish, so I told them the latest on Tiny and also about my parents moving away. They were both very supportive, and it definitely made me appreciate my wonderful friends. Time flew by, and I glanced down at my watch to see it was time to open my store. "See you guys later," I said waving as I headed next door.

I'd just put my petty cash in the drawer when the door chimed. It was Rochelle Copeland. I'd forgotten she was supposed to come in today. She'd stopped by a few days before asking if there were any job openings and as I was super busy that day, I asked her to come back early before the crowds started streaming in. "Hey, Ms. Rain!" she said smiling. She had a large tote on her shoulder bearing the image of a vampire.

"Hey, Rochelle! Come on in, and please, call me Averi." We'd hit it off the first time I talked with her and was actually anxious to see her work.

"Okay, Averi...I brought my portfolio of work to show you my designs," she said pulling out a binder. I flipped through it and was really impressed with them, some of which were very intricate. She also had some designs on her own hands, and I studied the line work and symmetry.

"These are great!" I said as I turned her hands. "You did this on yourself? I'm really impressed."

She grinned. "Yeah, I've always enjoyed art and that's what I consider this to be. I love tattoos but I also love that these fade and you can change them to something else later. By the way, I love the purple in your hair!"

"Thanks!" I said twirling one of the purple streaks in my fingers. "I had pink not too long ago for a wedding but decided on purple this time."

"I've wanted to do ombre on my hair but I'm not sure if I should," she said running her fingers through her own dark thick hair.

I grinned. "You know what? My hair stylist Stacey says, 'It's hair. If you don't like it, you can change it.' She's the one who gives me the courage to jump in and just do it."

"You'll have to give me her number. I think I'll give it a try."

Her personality was a perfect match for me and her portfolio was outstanding. I decided the way to test her technique was to let her do something on me. "Well, Rochelle, you really seem to have the touch and I'm going to let you show me by doing something special." I pulled out my sketch book and flipped to the one I was looking for. "Do you think you could do this one?"

She took the book and studied the pattern. "This is gorgeous!" She said running her fingers along the lines. "Do you have a client in mind for this?"

I grinned. "Yep. Me."

Her mouth fell open. "You? Are you sure?"

"Rochelle, I'm pretty confident you can handle it and I've been wanting a large piece for a while. Obviously, since it's a shoulder and side piece, it'd be impossible for me to do on my own."

She looked down at the picture again, took a deep breath and said, "Let's do it!"

I ran into the back to change into my bikini top and as I came back into the front, she was setting up her tools. "Would you rather have me sitting or lying down?" I asked.

"Um, I think for this, lying down will be better." I pulled out the table, laid a sheet on it and lay face down.

"Do you think you'll need a stencil?" I asked to see how proficient she was. Using a stencil for a very intricate henna was acceptable but really good artists could do it freehand.

As she mixed the henna paste, she looked over the design again. "I think I'd rather freehand this." I let her go for it, and thankfully, we weren't busy because it took about an hour and a half to do it. While she worked, we talked, and I learned that she'd moved from California to, as she put it, 'get away from earthquakes' and also an ex. She'd only been here a couple of months having started working her way down the coast trying her hand at different beach locations. She finally settled here after meeting a guy who worked at the marina, and they were sharing a place. "He's really nice and understands my bohemian side," she said laughing. I could tell she was getting close to finishing, and I was really excited to see it. She did a couple of swirls and then looked over the entire piece comparing it to the picture. "Okay, I think it's done!"

I climbed from the table, walked to the mirror and turned to look over my shoulder at my reflection. What I saw was more beautiful than I could have imagined. "Oh," was all I could say. My design, which consisted of the traditional henna swirls and dots started at my left shoulder, trailed down my back where it widened out then it wound its way back to end on my waist.

"Oh, as in 'Oh, this is fantastic' or Oh, as in 'Oh, this sucks!'" She asked with worry.

I smiled. "This is definitely fantastic! I love it and you are totally hired!"

The rest of the morning was pretty steady with the tourists getting their "vacation" hennas and having Rochelle there allowed me a break to take Tiny out every so often. He was so excited to see me, and it broke my heart to lock him right back up but it had been a busy day, and I needed to hurry back. About midday, I let Rochelle have a lunch break, and I flipped the sign to CLOSED to let me quickly gobble down a sandwich. As I came back out front, I saw some people leaning on the railing of the boardwalk watching the surfers, so I flipped over the sign on the door. I'd just gotten to the counter when I heard my door bell ring. The same people I'd seen outside came in and browsed around near the door at first then headed back toward me.

"May I help y'all?" I asked, as I quickly finished washing my hands.

As they approached, I could tell it was a father and daughter. They had matching olive complexions paired with jet black hair. The man spoke, "Yes, my daughter would like to get one of your henna tattoos but I just want to make sure it's safe before she does it."

I turned to his daughter who was giving me a dazzling smile. "My daddy worries too much, I'm an only child," she said laughing.

I laughed. "I feel your pain. I'm an only child too!"
Turning my attention to her father, I held up my hands to
show the delicate pattern I'd done only the day before.
"Sir, I can assure you that this is completely harmless. It's
a dye that marks the skin only temporarily. Within a
couple of weeks, it fades until it disappears completely. I
just got one today, as a matter of fact." I turned to show
my back piece and they both gasped. "Gorgeous, isn't it?
I promise you. She'll be fine. It's a lot better to do this than
get a permanent tattoo and regret it."

Turning the dazzling smile onto her dad, the young woman
pleaded, "Please, Daddy? You promised!"

Still looking at my hands, he said, "Okay, Brianna. You
pick out what you want. I think I'll grab a cup of coffee at
the shop next door. I'll leave you girls to it."

Brianna looked through the book of designs but kept
glancing at my hands. "My friend said I should get one on
my shoulder but honestly, I really like yours. Can you do
that for me?"

Nodding, I started gathering my supplies. "Sure thing,
have a seat and we'll get started."

She laughed. "You'll have to excuse my dad. He's very protective and probably visualizes my hands rotting off but I think seeing yours made him see that it's not so bad."

I joined in the laughter. "Yeah, mine haven't rotted off…yet!"

As I applied the pattern to her skin, I noticed her eyes. "You know, you're the first person I've ever met with the same eye color as me." Our eyes were deep chocolate brown with flecks of gold.

"That's so cool!" She gasped. "I wonder if we share a relative somewhere."

With a grin I said, "Ya know, we're probably cousins somewhere down the line."

She laughed. "We live in Nashville, Tennessee but my dad grew up in the area and we've been visiting some of his old stomping grounds. He went to high school here so he took me by and showed me the field where he played football."

I smiled. "I'm sure it's the same school I graduated from. It's been the only one around here for over forty years and it hasn't changed much over the years, just a few more coats of paint."

We were just about finished when her dad came back in. He walked up behind Brianna and resting his hands on her shoulders, leaned over to see her hands. "I think I'm almost done," Brianna said smiling. "I love it so much! Don't you Daddy?"

He rolled his eyes and smiled. "If you love it, then I do."

I applied the last swirl and started wiping off my tools. "Okay, she's done and ready to go. That'll be twenty dollars." I stepped over to the cash register and a thought hit me. "So, your daughter tells me you grew up and graduated here. My mom is probably close to your age, what year did you graduate?

"A long time ago," he said laughing, "1994, to be exact. What was her name?" He pulled out his wallet and started sifting through his cash.

I rang up the sale as I answered. "Well, her name is Charlotte but when she was younger, everyone called her Lottie, her maiden name was Smith."

He froze and didn't say anything, just stood motionless. It actually freaked me out for a minute then he said, "Lottie…yes, I knew Lottie." He shook his head slightly then abruptly turned to Brianna and said, "Well, we'd better get going. Your mom will wonder what happened to us." He put a fifty down on the counter and said, "Keep the change. Thank you for doing such a beautiful job."

Shocked, I picked up the money and gave him a huge smile. "Well, thank you and if you know of anyone else who'd like one, please recommend our shop. My name's Averi and I appreciate referrals."

He put his arm tightly around his daughter's shoulders as they walked out. His reaction seemed strange, so I made a mental note to ask my mom if she knew him, then realized I'd never asked his name. Oh well, it wasn't important anyway. I checked the clock and saw it was closing time. I locked up and headed up to the apartment. Tiny was so happy to be free from his crate, and since it was a mild night, I loaded him up in my Jeep and headed to Ft. Fisher to walk him around the park. As he sniffed every blade of grass and barked at the seagulls, I breathed in the salty air and gazed at the sky which was now filled with the vibrant colors of sunset. I was getting back in the Jeep when my phone chimed with a text from my parents. They were safely in Boone and sent me a slightly out of focus selfie of them in front of their new place. Smiling, I saved the picture and made it the screensaver on my phone.

I drove back to the apartment and walking up the steps, I saw something in front of the door. As I got closer, I could see it was a bouquet of flowers. Naturally, I expected they were from Alex as an apology but was surprised when I opened the card.

Tiny,

Hope these brighten your day! You can share them with your mommy, if you want to…

Uncle Ian

Laughing, I picked up the gorgeous arrangement of sunflowers before Tiny could sample any of the blooms. Setting them on the kitchen counter where I could admire them, I fed the bottomless pit that was panting by my leg, and then I re-read the card. I really shouldn't have been so happy to get flowers from someone other than my boyfriend, but they really came at a time I needed them. Kicking my shoes off, I threw on my jammies and curled up on the futon which had now become my favorite spot in the apartment. My phone chimed, and I saw a message from Alex.

Got called in to work again. I'll come by tomorrow night, if that's good for you.

I still found it odd that I hadn't seen him much since Ian left, but I knew how busy his job could be at times. Feeling pangs of guilt, I texted back.

Sounds good. I'll order pizza. Do you know what time?

A few minutes passed then a reply.

I'll just have to let you know. Talk to you tomorrow. Goodnight.

As I read his reply, it struck me how impersonal his messages were. No hot sexting here. I picked up the card from my flowers, and I could just picture Ian's face as he was writing it. I scooped Tiny up from the floor, and he settled across my lap on the futon. I scrolled through the channels and found an old movie. Within minutes, I could feel my eyelids becoming heavy. I was just about to drift off when I heard my phone ring. Sleepily, I answered without looking to see who it was.

"Hey, sleepyhead!" When I heard Ian's voice I couldn't help but smile.

"Hey, yourself!"

"So, did Tiny like the flowers I sent?" He asked chuckling.

I smiled broadly. "Yes, he did and he was nice enough to share them with me." My eyes wandered over to the bouquet and I could just imagine the person writing the card when he ordered them.

He laughed out loud. "What a good boy!" He paused then said, "Seriously, I hope they made your day a little brighter."

"Yeah, they did," I admitted. "That was very thoughtful of you."

"Not a problem," he said softly. "I love to make you smile."

My face flushed, and I was thankful he couldn't see how he affected me. Changing the subject quickly, I asked, "So, when are you due back?"

"As far as I know, we're supposed to be headed back at the end of the week. You've still got a few more days to miss me," he said laughing.

"Oh thank God. Tiny and I are enjoying having the apartment all to ourselves."

"Well, I'm sure Alex has been keeping you company too, right?" he asked, and I cringed. Did I really want to admit how lonely I'd been?

Sighing, I told him the truth. "Not really. He's been busy at work."

"Oh man! You mean I could have had you all to myself? My life sucks!"

I waited for the teasing laugh, but it never came. "Ian, you shouldn't say things like that. He's my boyfriend and whether he's here or not, that's the way it is." I tried to sound convincing, but it fell flat.

Not missing a beat, he said, "Hey, a guy can dream, right?"

I ignored his comment and again changed the subject. "Well, it's getting late and I need to get up early for work. You take care, okay?" I absently scratched Tiny behind the ear as I again closed my eyes to imagine Ian cuddling with us.

"I will and I'll see you soon. Goodnight, Little Bit." I heard the phone disconnect, and I laid it down on the table.

Tiny crawled up my chest to nibble on my nose. I pulled him away and watched as his legs paddled the air trying to reach me. "Why does he do this to me?" I asked out loud. "Why can't I just shut him out of my heart?" Tiny just whimpered and licked his lips. "You're not helping me," I laughed. I hugged him close to my chest, and he happily chewed on the ends of my hair. I pulled a throw from the back of the futon to cover us, and we were soon fast asleep.

Chapter 8

Ian

I hung up the phone after speaking with Averi and smiled as I finished packing my clothes. It was the hardest thing to keep it secret that Tristan and I were heading back early, but I wanted it to be a surprise. Hearing that she hadn't seen much of Alex all week was a definite bonus. The man had to be a complete idiot not to want to spend every moment with Averi. Of course, this was making things easier for me.

I was waiting for the bellhop, so I had the door of my room ajar. Tristan, whose room was across the hall knocked then walked in carrying his bags. "You about ready to roll?" he asked eyeing my half-packed bag. "What have you been doing? You know the flight leaves in a few hours and we've got to get through a ton of traffic to get there."

"Yeah, sorry. I was talking to Averi. I should be done in just a few minutes," I said shoving my shoes in wherever they'd fit.

He sat down in the chair near the bed. "Averi? She's actually talking to you?" he asked with a smirk.

I shrugged. "I guess she's slowly coming around. My mojo is hard to resist," I said with a big cheesy smile. "It's in the genes, bro. We can't deny it."

Tristan nodded solemnly. "Yes, it is a blessed curse. Kendall couldn't resist me. It's a fact. I guess I just find it hard to believe that knowing all she knows about you that she'd even talk to you, never mind live with you. You have to admit, Ian. Your past was pretty…how can I say this nicely…extensive? You can't go anywhere without running into someone you've got some sort of past with."

I couldn't deny what he said, it was all true. "I admit, I've had my fair share but contrary to everyone's belief, I didn't sleep with everyone I dated. I think my reputation got to the point that even if I didn't sleep with someone, everyone assumed I did. I'm not proud of my past but I honestly think that was to show me what I really want and that's Averi. Tristan, I want what you have. I want to wake up with her every morning, go home to her every day and sleep with her every night…the whole package." I finished zipping my bag and slapped him on the shoulder.

"Everybody deserves a chance to redeem themselves and I'm just hoping that Averi will give me one."

The bellhop knocked and rolled the cart in to get our luggage. Tristan stood, grabbed his laptop bag and smiling said, "Let's go home to our women."

We arrived in Wilmington right before six in the morning after a very long flight. Tristan's truck was at the airport, so he dropped me off then headed home determined to slip into bed and surprise his still sleeping wife. As I approached the building, I saw a light on in the window of our apartment. It was so early, I could only assume she'd been awakened by the puppy. I quietly crept up the stairs, and as I got closer to the door, I could hear someone singing. I listened for a moment and recognized the words of the song as 'Still Into You' by one of my favorite bands, Paramore. Averi was singing at the top of her lungs, and I stood listening at the door with a smile on my face. Carefully, I unlocked it and peeped through the crack. She was in the kitchen with her back to me, her hair up in her usual messy bun. Holding a wooden spoon as a microphone, she bobbed her head and danced along with the music. Her free hand was waving in the air with the beat of the music. I eased the door open, set my bag down then carefully closed the door, determined not to disturb this performance. She had her eyes closed, a huge smile on her face. I leaned back against the door, crossed my arms and enjoyed the show taking in how beautiful she was. The song was almost over when she spun around and opened her eyes. She froze in place, a look of pure horror on her flushed face.

"Oh my God! You scared me to death!" she shouted over the blaring music. She turned it down then stalked over to me. "Exactly how long have you been standing there? And what are you doing home anyway?"

I looked into her dark brown eyes rimmed with long, silky lashes and felt myself go weak. "Miss me?" I asked trying to restrain myself from kissing those lush lips before carrying her to the bedroom to show her how much I missed her.

She lowered her eyes. "Well, it was quiet around here, I must admit."

I cradled her chin with my fingers to lift her gaze to mine. "So, it was quiet. Is that the only thing different while I was gone?" I wanted to hear her say she missed me. I needed to hear it.

She swallowed hard then backed away from my grasp and ran to the bedroom door. "Well, I do have something to show you." She opened the door and a super-sized puppy galloped out, his tongue lolling and tail wagging.

He ran to me and began tugging on my pant leg with his sharp white teeth. "This can't be the same dog! I was only gone just over a week!" He'd doubled in size and had already lost some of the roundness of a puppy. "Averi…what kind of dog is he again?"

She fidgeted and bit her bottom lip, which was just adorable but was also distracting my focus. "Well, I really don't know." She was being evasive, and I had a gut feeling she knew exactly what kind of dog he was.

"Averi, is he by any chance a Great Dane?" I asked as I watched him carry around one of her flip flops. He lay down and wrapped his paws around it as he gnawed on the sole. It was at that moment that I noticed his enormous paws. "Wow, look at those feet! If his feet are any indication, he's going to be a horse!"

Quickly, she bent down to pull the flip flop from his mouth and exchanged a rawhide for it. He never missed a beat and began working on it as heartily as he had the flip flop. "He's possibly a Great Dane," she said with a wince. "I just know he needed a home and I love him. If you don't feel you can live with that, I understand."

My heart sank. She actually believed that would make me leave. She still didn't get how I felt about her. At that moment, I made a decision. No more chasing her. It was time to back off the pressure and let her come to me. It was a pretty risky move, and it may be the biggest mistake I ever make, but I was relying on my instincts. I stood silently for a moment, then shrugged. "No, I'm good. Since I need a place to stay, I'll just live with it."

A puzzled look came over her face. "You're sure?"

I nodded then picked up my bag. "Yeah, it's cool." I rummaged through my bag and casually tossed a ball to Tiny. Glancing out the window at the sun rising over the water, I said, "Well, I think I'm going to change and catch some waves since I've got the rest of the week off." I left her standing there looking dumbfounded. I wanted to spend every moment I could with her, but it was time to be tough in order to win her heart forever.

Resisting the urge to go home, I spent the rest of the day hanging down on the beach, riding some waves and catching up with some of the guys I used to hang with. A couple of them were now working at the fire department, so

I casually asked if they knew anything about Alex. They both told me that he had quite the reputation with the ladies. Trying to act nonchalant, I asked, "Isn't he dating just one girl right now? That's what I'd heard."

Laughing, my friend said, "One per day, maybe! Let me tell you, Ian…the uniform is a chick magnet. Alex sure knows how to use it too! He's got ladies all over town and on the nights he's not working, he's working it somewhere! No different from you, my friend. In fact, you're a legend around town."

Shame washed over me as I realized they idolized me for being a dog. Alex was just another version of me, rolling from one conquest to another. "Well, I'm trying to change my ways, fellas," I said picking up my board. "When you've found the one, then you need to make her your one and only focus. Life's too short." I left them with their mouths hanging open and headed back to the apartment. Averi was still at work, so I took a shower. After drying off and taking Tiny outside for a walk, I came back in and started cooking dinner.

One of the advantages of having an Irish mother was that she knew how to cook and since I'd always been hanging out in the kitchen with her, it rubbed off on me. I dug through the kitchen and found all of the ingredients to make an Irish Shepherd's pie. After putting it all together, I slid it into the oven to brown the top then set the table for two. I heard Averi coming up the stairs and when she opened the door, I saw her eyes widen with surprise.

"What have you done?" she asked, her eyes taking in the candlelit table as she sniffed deeply. "It smells amazing!"

"I made you and Alex dinner," I said pulling the casserole from the oven to set it on the table. "I figure he'll be here shortly so it's all ready." I walked past her and grabbed my keys and wallet. "I hope you enjoy it. It's one of my mom's recipes."

She stood staring at me. "Are you leaving?"

I nodded. "Yeah, you and your guy deserve some time alone."

I had my hand on the knob when I heard her phone chime. She glanced down at it and frowned. "Well, thanks for making dinner, but it looks like I'll be eating by myself. Alex just cancelled. He got called into work."

The conversation I'd had with the guys was fresh in my mind. I had a feeling that it wasn't work but someone else entertaining him tonight, but I kept that information to myself since I had no proof. I made a mental note to do some checking up on Alex and his mysterious activities.

My thoughts were interrupted by Averi waving her hand in front of my face. "I said do you want to eat dinner with me? Or are you going out?"

I studied her face. "Do *you* want me to stay?"

She smiled. "Yes, I'd like you to join me. You went to all this trouble, you should eat." She walked over to the table and sat down. I threw my keys on the counter and sat across from her. "I'm still amazed you did this!" she said taking a deep sniff. "I had no idea you knew how to cook."

I picked up the dish and spooned out a portion onto her plate. "Yeah, I picked it up while watching my mom do her thing in the kitchen. She's an amazing cook." After dishing out my own portion, I poured us both a glass of wine. Lifting my glass, I said, "Cheers!" Smiling, she clinked her glass to mine.

As we ate, our conversation was sociable but after a couple of glasses of wine, she loosened up and the walls came down. She laughed and flirted, and I loved seeing that side of her. As we finished our meal, I got up to put the dishes in the sink. I began to run the water and turned to find Averi leaning against the counter right next to me.

"Can I ask you a question?" she said looking up at me. When I nodded, she continued. "Why are you here, Ian?" she asked before taking a big gulp of her wine. "What do you want from me?" Her body pressed against mine.

I played coy. "I don't know what you mean. I want to be your friend. What do you think I want?" For the first time, I saw something I'd never seen before in her eyes, desire. I had to swallow hard when I saw her pink tongue dart out to lick her lips. Her eyes were hooded, her breath shallow. I brushed a loose tendril of hair back from her dark chocolate eyes to tuck it behind her ear. I saw her shiver as she brushed her cheek against my palm. "Averi," I said softly, "I want what you want." I leaned into her and felt her body tremble.

Taking a deep breath, she was about to speak when we were interrupted by a knock at the door. "Who is it?" she shouted. She was definitely feeling the wine.

A feminine voice on the other side of the door said, "Excuse me…does Ian O'Neal live here?" Averi's face instantly clouded over.

I moved toward the door to get rid of whoever it was quickly, but despite the wine, she was faster. She whipped open the door and with her hand on her hip said, "Who wants to know?"

Standing out of view of the door, I heard the girl say, "My name's Ricki and we hung out last summer. My family's in town and I ran into a friend of his who told me how to find him. I thought I'd stop by and see if he wanted to hang out." Averi stood staring at her. After an awkward silence, Ricki continued, "Um, who are you? His sister or something?"

I saw Averi's jaw clench. "Why would you think that I'm his sister? Am I not hot enough to be his girlfriend? Is that what you think?" She took a step toward her. "I'll have you know that I am *not* his sister." She looked back at me. "You have company." She swung the door open and turned and walked to her bedroom. "Remember our agreement, Ian," she said over her shoulder.

"Look," Ricki said, "I don't know what your deal is with her but I came here to have some fun."

Taking her arm, I walked her down the stairs fighting off her hands the entire time. As we reached the boardwalk, I said, "Listen, I appreciate your stopping by but I'm not into hooking up," I said. "I'm trying to have a real relationship and leave that behind. I think it's best if you leave."

"Fine! Be that way! I'll find someone else…I don't need you!" she huffed as she snatched her arm from my grip. I watched as she marched down the boardwalk until she was out of sight. I turned to open the door to the building and almost ran into Alex.

"Well," I said with a wry smile, "look who's here. I could've sworn Averi said you had to work tonight."

He shifted uneasily. "Um, another guy came in and since Averi was *really* disappointed that I'd had to work, I came as soon as she texted me."

"When was that?" I asked curiously.

"Just a few minutes ago, if you must know. I happened to be in the area," he said abruptly.

Suddenly, an old saying hit me. 'Keep your friends close and your enemies closer.' I changed my approach. "Hey man, I know we really didn't hit it off but I just want you to know that I'm only living here because my brother lost a bet. There's nothing going on with between us and from the way she feels about me, I know there never would be."

He stopped in mid-step. "So you're saying this is just for convenience? Just for a place to live? You have no interest in Averi, at all?"

I looked him dead in the eye and lied my ass off. "Nah man, I'm gonna be headed out in a few to meet up with the girl that just left. I have no interest in Averi."

Apparently, I was pretty convincing because he smiled. "Good, and let's keep it that way. By the way, her name was Ricki, right?"

I nodded. "Yeah she's a hot one, but I guess I don't have to tell you that, huh?"

He gave me a knowing nod. "Oh yeah, she's hot!"

I clapped him on the shoulder. "My man, it looks like we've been going about this the wrong way. We're more alike than we realized."

He smiled. "Well, I'll never have the rep you have but I'm working on it. Just between us, I'm trying to get Averi to loosen up. It's been slow going but I think it'll pay off soon."

I wanted to punch the smile right off his face, but instead I gritted my teeth in a weird grin. "Here's hoping!"

We entered the apartment, and he went to the bedroom door. He knocked softly. "Averi, it's me Alex."

The door cracked, and I saw her holding Tiny. I rushed forward and said, "Here, let me take him for a walk."

I could see the hurt in her eyes and knew that Ricki coming to our door had once again ruined a beautiful moment. Obviously, it bothered her enough to text Alex. I took Tiny from her arms leaving them alone for a while but while I was out walking, I was plotting my next move.

Chapter 9

Averi

What was I thinking? I asked myself this over and over as I listened to Alex talk about himself and try to make out with me. We sat on my bed watching a DVD in my portable player and when he tried to kiss me, I coughed and sniffled pretending to have a cold coming on. All I could think of was Ian and how I wished he was here instead of him. Finally, after yawning several times, he got the hint and went home. I peeked out and saw that neither Ian nor Tiny were in the apartment. I put on my windbreaker and a pair of shoes and wandered outside to find them walking along the boardwalk.

"So, Alex went home?" He asked looking around.

I nodded. "Yeah, it's late and I have to work tomorrow. I also told him it wasn't fair for you to have to walk the beach all night."

He laughed. "Actually, we've enjoyed ourselves. Tiny made friends with a poodle who was also out for an evening walk."

There was an awkward silence. "I'm sorry I reacted the way I did when your friend came over," I said trying not to look him in the eye. "I guess the wine went to my head." I reached down to scratch Tiny's ear.

He touched the side of my face, forcing me to look at him. "Averi, I told her that she wasn't welcome. She won't be back." As the shivers from his touch ran through my body, I pulled my jacket tightly around me, pretending the ocean breeze had been the cause. Suddenly, he pulled his hand back and stuck it in his pocket. To hide my disappointment, I turned away and started walking toward home. He quickly caught up with me and silently, we strolled back upstairs. Once inside, I told him goodnight and went to my bedroom. Having spent the better part of a week on the futon, I really felt out of place in my own bed. I curled into a ball, replaying the events of the evening. Was I misreading Ian or was he really into me? I felt so confused. Tiny walked across the bed to snuggle closer to me. Despite having a larger area to sleep in, he ended up lying across me, his hot puppy breath right in my face. His rhythmic breathing lulled me to sleep, and before I knew it, the sun was streaming in my window.

I crept out of my room and found Ian was already gone, his futon neatly made and a note on the counter.

Working a lifeguard shift. Will call you later to see what your plans are for tonight so I won't intrude.

Having consumed way too much wine, I had the morning after headache, and I really didn't feel like going to work. I struggled to get downstairs in time to open. I had to skip my coffee, so I was not in the best of moods when I got to the store. I was putting my key in the lock when I noticed an envelope halfway under the door. I pushed the door open then picked it up. AVERI was neatly printed across the plain white envelope. I backed out the door and looked around but didn't see anyone nearby so I tucked it under my arm until I could put my stuff down. After getting everything set up for the day, I turned my attention to the mysterious envelope. As I tore it open, I could see it was several handwritten pages. I slid it out and as I started to read, I felt myself go numb.

Averi,

Let me start by saying if you don't want to read this, I would completely understand, but I hope you'll hang in here and read this entire letter. I'm counting on your curiosity to let me explain why I felt compelled to write this.

My name is Gordon, and you met my daughter Brianna and me the other day. I must apologize for my strange behavior when you mentioned your mom. I knew your mom very well, and it shook me up when I realized you were her daughter.

I met your mom, Lottie when we were both in high school. We were both seventeen. I was on the football team, and she was a cheerleader so naturally we were thrown together in social situations. She was the most popular girl in school, and every guy wanted to date her…but she chose me. We'd been dating a few months when suddenly, right after graduation, she broke up with me. She never gave me an explanation, just told me not to call or try to see her. I respected her wishes even though I was hurt and confused. Later that fall, right before I went to college, I ran into her in town. I knew it was her right away. She was standing with her back to me and as I called her name, she turned and I saw she now had a very obvious baby bump. After doing some quick calculations in my head, I assumed the baby was mine and asked her point blank, but she made it very clear that it wasn't. It hurt to think that she'd been with someone else, but that made it easier for me to move on. I attended college that fall, eventually relocated out of state to start my career after graduation, and went on with my life.

Seventeen years ago, I met a wonderful woman. We married and had Brianna a year later. Honestly, when I met you, I was struck by how much you resembled my own daughter even having our unique eye color, but as soon as you told me who your mother was, I knew she'd misled me all those years ago and that you are, in fact, my daughter.

The point of this letter is this. I want a chance to get to know you. I'd just like to meet and talk, I'm not asking for anything more. I'll be here for another week. If I don't hear from you, I'll leave you alone and never contact you again. My number is on the enclosed card.

Sincerely,

Gordon Haynes

The letter fell from my hand, and I found myself dropping into a chair to stop the room from spinning. This couldn't be true. My first instinct was to call my mom, but then I realized I had no idea what to say. First and foremost, I needed to calm down and breathe. I could feel an anxiety attack coming on so I dropped my head between my knees and tried to slow my breathing. After a few minutes, I felt a bit calmer so with trembling hands, I picked up the letter again and re-read it. As much as I wanted to dismiss it, I couldn't deny the fact that we all had the same jet black hair, the same olive complexion and Brianna and I shared the same unusual eyes. My mom was blonde and petite with bright green eyes, the exact opposite to my coloring. My dad had dark brown hair and…green eyes. I sat down at the computer and did a search using genetics and eye color and found that it was impossible for two green-eyed people to have a brown-eyed child. I felt a knot form in my gut. This was definitely probable. My phone rang, and I jumped out of my skin. It was Alex.

"Hey," I said clearing my throat trying to sound normal. "What's up?"

"Hang on," he covered his phone, and I could hear muffled voices then he came back, "sorry, I'm at work. I got called in to cover someone's shift who's sick."

"So that means you're not coming over?" I said with a relieved sigh.

He paused. "Well, no but you don't have to sound so happy about it."

I hadn't realized how loud that sigh had been. "Um, no Alex. I'm not happy. Can't a girl sigh because her boyfriend stood her up again?"

He bought it. "Oh okay, that's more like it. I'm sorry again and I'll try to make it up to you, soon." The voices in the background got louder, and he again covered the phone. Quickly, he said, "Hey I gotta go. Night!"

I felt badly that I was so relieved he wasn't coming over, but I really didn't want to face him tonight. I needed time to absorb this bombshell of a letter *and* hopefully talk to my mom. Setting my phone down on the counter, it vibrated showing a text from Ian.

Just checking in. Do I need to disappear tonight?

Did I want Ian to be home? Yes, for some weird reason, I did. He seemed to be the only one I could really talk to lately. Just the thought of being around him soothed me.

No, you can come home. Alex is working, I texted back.

He responded immediately.

Awesome, I'll make you another of my famous dinners.

I laid my phone down on the counter and picked up the letter again. I was glancing over it when some customers came in so I quickly tucked it into my bag. The rest of the day was spent doing some henna and a couple of ear piercings. I tried to get a hold of Kendall to talk, but her co-worker Becky told me she was at an appointment. By the time I closed up shop, I was exhausted both mentally and physically. I dragged myself up to the apartment, and as I approached the door, the most delicious aroma greeted me. I opened the door to find Ian shirtless wearing my 'Kiss the Cook' apron in the middle of the kitchen. He turned and gave me a huge smile.

"Hungry?" he asked. "I'm just about finished. The bread should be ready in just a few minutes." He handed me a glass of wine.

I stood slack-jawed watching him move around the kitchen. I'd had one of the weirdest days and he'd just made it a lot better. "Thank you," was all I could say.

He looked at me closely then tilted his head. "Are you okay?" he asked walking over to stand directly in front of me. "You look like you've got something on your mind."

I blurted, "Ian, I don't want to talk about it, okay?"

Surprised at my outburst, he nodded slowly. "Okay…but I'm here if you need me."

I took a big swallow of my wine. "Thank you…for everything." I set my glass down and went into my room to change. I put on some shorts and a t-shirt and wandered back out just as he was putting the food on the table. I looked around for Tiny and found he was fast asleep on the futon, his feet twitching as he was obviously chasing something good in his dreams. Ian pulled out my chair then helped me scoot to the table. He'd made hearty Irish stew with fresh crusty bread and after refilling my wine, he removed his apron, slipped on a tank top, much to my disappointment, and sat down across from me. The food was so delicious and so was the view. "So, how was your day?" I asked taking a bite of the tender beef dripping in gravy.

He looked up in surprise. "Uh, well…good. I worked a shift on the beach and got a phone call from the office. It turns out, I'm getting a promotion."

"Wow! Congratulations!" Smiling, I held up my glass for a toast. "Wishing you the best of luck in your new job!" He lifted his glass to mine.

"Thanks," he said returning the smile. "I did some errands and then decided to cook for you since you seemed to like my culinary skills."

"Like them? I love them!" I said as I speared a big chunk of potato. "Plus, any food I don't have to cook is even better."

He leaned back in his chair and laughed. "Oh, so I do have a purpose here after all. Glad I could be of service, ma'am." His ice blue eyes were sparkling with amusement as he leaned toward me. "Is there anything else I can do for you?" His tone became suggestive, his voice deeper. Instantly, my heart started racing like it had that night he'd kissed me. Then just as quickly, he stood and started clearing the dishes. I was shocked and a bit confused watching as he put them in the sink then started running the water to wash them.

Taking another huge swallow of wine, I jumped up from the table and tried to nonchalantly grab a towel to hide my trembling hands. "I'll dry," I said grabbing a dish from the drying rack. We worked in silence and when we were finished, he grabbed his keys.

"I'm going out for a while," he said as he opened the door. "Have a nice evening. Call me if you need anything."

The silence in the apartment was deafening after he left. I grabbed the bottle of wine and my glass then threw myself onto the futon. I reached into my bag to pull out the letter that had rocked my world. I read it again, and so many questions were coming to my mind about what happened twenty-one years ago. Nursing my glass, I lay there thinking back through all of my childhood memories, and they were only happy ones, nothing out of the ordinary. Tiny grunted as he moved to sprawl over my legs literally locking me in place. My mind was buzzing with the combination of wine and the shock of the letter. I set the wine glass on the floor, curled into a ball and promptly passed out.

I felt myself being lifted from the futon and instinctively, I held on tight. The warm breath against my cheek was soothing, and I snuggled closer, pulling myself in even tighter. I was lowered onto my bed but didn't want to let go so I held on. I heard a murmur and a sigh then felt the bed sink with our weight. Arms wrapped around me pulling me closer, warm breath now on the back of my neck lulling me back into sleep. The strong arms began to release me, but I held on tight. "Don't leave me," I mumbled and felt a kiss on the back of my neck as a warm hand slid under my shirt to rest on my stomach. If this was a dream, I didn't want it to end. Suddenly, I felt something cold touch my hand causing me to jump. Startled, I opened my eyes and realized I was all alone except for my puppy who was nudging my hand with his nose. My head throbbing from my second hangover, I vowed to lay off the wine, threw my arm over my eyes and groaned. It had all been a dream.

Chapter 10

Ian

I left to go running early so I wouldn't embarrass her. I knew it was the wine talking when she asked me to stay and despite my best efforts to leave her alone, I couldn't resist having her in my arms. The scent of her hair, the softness of her skin, all were irresistible to me, and I found myself wanting more. The old Ian would have taken advantage of her vulnerability, but that wasn't the kind of relationship I wanted with her. I also wasn't going to be the 'other man' to Alex. She needed to know what kind of cheating ass he was, and I had to figure out how to make that happen. As soon as she'd fallen asleep, I'd eased myself off the bed and tiptoed from the room, leaving her gently snoring.

As I took a break on the beach to watch the first of the beachgoers setting up their chairs, I mulled over how exactly to get Averi to catch Alex red-handed. I called one of my buddies at the fire station and casually asked about

Alex's work schedule. "Do you guys cover for each other a lot?"

"Rarely," he said laughing. "We have more than enough guys even if someone has to be off. Chief doesn't like us switching around anyway. If we start screwing around with the schedule, he'll kick our asses." I could hear him flipping some papers. "Looks like Alex is off for two more days."

Using that information, I devised a plan to catch the player at his own game. "Hey, do you happen to have his phone number?" I asked my friend who promptly gave it to me.

Averi was at work so I dashed back to the apartment to change then dialed Alex's number. It rang several times, and I was just about to hang up when I heard him answer warily, "Hello?"

"Hey, Alex, it's Ian!"

"Um, hey." He sounded suspicious and rightly so. "What's up?"

"Well, I was going grab a beer at the Junction and thought maybe you'd be up for a game or two of pool."

He hesitated for a moment then said, "Okay, sure." Then he added, "But don't tell Averi because I'm supposed to be working tonight."

"Oh, sure, no problem. Your secret's safe with me. What she doesn't know…right?"

He laughed. "Yeah, honestly, I can't stand that dog drooling all over me so I find any excuse I can to avoid going over there."

"Hey, I know what you mean…I've gotta live there," I said, chuckling trying to sound sincere. "Why don't you take her out sometime? I can watch the dog for her."

"Ah, man. I can't do that. I might run into someone I know, if you catch my drift. That wouldn't be cool, at all. It's easier to hang out at her place."

I tried to keep my voice calm, but I wanted to jump through the phone and pound his face in. "Man, I don't know why you bother when you've got so many other options. That's way too complicated for me," I asked trying not to clench my teeth.

He must not have noticed my clipped tone. "Dude, I know you don't think of her that way but damn, she's got a banging body and I'm not giving up yet."

I was clenching my hand so tightly around my phone that I thought it would shatter. "Yeah," I said coolly. "I guess she's okay. I've known her since high school so I've seen her at her geekiest. Kinda puts a damper on her hotness for me but hey, whatever turns you on."

He laughed again, and I clenched my free hand into a fist. "Oh well she definitely turns me on. I just can't figure out what she's waiting for."

I needed to end this conversation before I broke my phone. "Well, give her some time," I found myself saying.

"Yeah, I'll give her time…I've got plenty of options in the meantime." He paused then said, "I need to jump in the shower, can meet you in about an hour?"

"Sure, see you then." I hung up the phone then headed out.

The Junction was just getting busy from the after work crowd, and as soon as I walked in, I noticed several young women drinking at the bar. Avoiding them, for now, I flagged the bartender down at the end of the bar, ordered a beer and found a table near the pool tables. Alex sauntered in about a half an hour later and his eyes immediately locked onto the selection of ladies. His eyes then scanned the pool tables and seeing me, he gave me a nod. Instead of avoiding the group of ladies like a good boyfriend should, he went right in between them to order his beer.

Sitting back in my chair, I watched him work the crowd with eye contact, 'accidental touches' and flirtatious greetings. He was really good at it, obviously he'd had a lot of practice. He eventually worked his way over to our table, and I couldn't help but notice several ladies had picked up their drinks and relocated to a table nearby.

"Hey man, you ready to lose?" he asked with a smirk and a quick glance to make sure his audience was watching. His cocky attitude was making me sick but I kept my cool.

I shook my head and laughed. "Looks like someone needs to be schooled," I said as I racked up the balls. Out of the corner of my eye, I noticed the ladies moving in even closer. Alex made the opening break, and a lone solid colored ball dropped in a pocket.

"Guess you get stripes," he said lining up his next shot which he easily knocked in. I leaned against the table taking a sip of my beer and letting him have plenty of room for his shots. He finally missed a shot and it was my turn. After our conversation earlier about Averi, I wanted to beat him so badly in front of our audience, but I took a deep breath and missed a shot I could have made easily. He finished knocking his balls in and gave the ladies a dazzling smile.

"Too bad we didn't bet anything," I said pulling the balls back out onto the table. He nodded then reached into his back pocket to pull out his wallet.

He fished around, pulled out a hundred and slapped it down on the table. "You're right…is this too rich for you?" There were murmurs from the crowd who'd gathered to watch us play. The attention he was getting just egged him on. "I mean, I can spot you a hundred if you don't have it on you."

Shrugging, I laughed. "That's okay," I said pulling out my wallet. "I can hang with you." I set my matching hundred next to his.

A gorgeous blonde stepped toward us and as she passed behind Alex, she trailed her hand around his waist. "Do you boys need me to hang on to your money for you?" she purred. She looked straight at Alex when she said it making it obvious she was interested.

"Sounds good," I said picking up the money to hand it to her. She suggestively slid her hand over mine as she took the money then tucked it into the lacy red bra that was barely covered by her black tank top. The flash from a diamond studded wedding band on her hand caught my eye. Seeing my eyes on her, she slowly licked her lips then picked up Alex's beer to take a drink.

"You don't mind, do you?" She was holding the bottle right next to her lips, and Alex was captivated.

Swallowing hard, he said, "You know sharing a drink is almost like kissing…almost."

Dropping her hand around his shoulder, she nuzzled his neck then nibbled on his earlobe. "Nothing's like the real thing," she growled.

They were so engrossed in each other that when I made the opening break, they never even noticed. I made two balls on the first shot, and both were stripes, so I called them and then began to run the table. Alex stood watching with his mouth slightly agape. I noticed the blonde was now watching with interest. It was a really easy table, and I knocked the balls in one after another until just the nine ball remained. Alex was visibly shaken by the ease with which I wiped the table clean, and as I called the final pocket, he flinched at the crack of the ball and the subsequent thump of it falling home.

The blonde appeared torn between her seduction of Alex and the seduction of my two hundred dollars. When I held out my hand for the money, her face fell, but she took her time removing it from her bra before handing it to me. When she didn't get a reaction from me, she turned her attention back to him.

I was still in earshot when I heard Alex say to her, "Let me give you my address." He wrote something down on a napkin and slipped it into the back pocket of her jeans, his hand lingering there deliberately. "Perfect, my husband leaves town tomorrow. I'll come over after eight and we'll finish this." She touched her lips to his then as she broke the kiss, she bit down on his lower lip tugging on it gently. With a suggestive squeeze on his butt, she turned and walked out.

"Whew, I know what I'll be doing tomorrow night," he said giving me a thumbs up. "Married women are worth the risk. I may have lost the bet but I got the girl."

I gave him a nod and returned the thumbs up. "Go for it, Romeo," I said with a forced laugh. The idiot was making this too easy for me. Tomorrow night, the next phase of my plan would begin.

When I got home later that night, Averi was already in bed and the next morning, she left before I got up. I started a huge pot of chili and totally cleaned the apartment from top to bottom. It was almost too much to handle when I went to clean up the bathroom and found Averi's lacy underwear hanging from the shower curtain rod. Obviously, she'd assumed she'd have time to get them down before I got home. Picturing her wearing the black lacy bra and panties literally made me lose my breath. Averi had some wicked curves, and I loved every one of them. I deliberately left them hanging there knowing she'd figure out I'd been in there.

I was just finishing up the dishes when she came upstairs. Her face showed surprise when she saw me home before her, and she rushed past me to the bathroom, her face flushed with embarrassment. She came out with her things tucked under her arm. "Um, I'm sorry I didn't get all of my stuff out of the bathroom," she stammered. "I didn't expect you until later."

I shrugged with indifference. "It's no biggie. I've seen you in your bikinis but I think I prefer the lace." Turning my back to her, I stirred the chili. "Hey, I made some chili for dinner and I have way too much. How'd you like to invite Alex over?"

She sighed. "Okay," she said before mumbling to herself, "I doubt he'll come." She picked up her phone, texted a message and within a minute, she got a reply. Shaking her head, she frowned. "Nope. He's got to work."

My plan was working. Now it was time for my innocent push. "Hey, I bet he and the guys down at the station would like some dinner. You should take them a big bowl. I'll fix it up for you."

She hesitated. "Well, I don't want to bother him at work. I should ask if it's okay." She picked up her phone, but I took it from her.

"Averi, this is a perfect way to surprise him. Plus the guys at the station will appreciate it too!" I grabbed some Tupperware and spooned several helpings into the bowl and popped a lid on it.

Reluctantly, she took the bowl, grabbed her keys and with a glance over her shoulder, she left.

I waited about five minutes then headed out to follow her. She'd jumped in her Jeep and was headed across town to the station. I managed to blend into traffic a few cars behind her. Parking across the street in an alley, I was able to keep an eye on what was going down. Carefully balancing the bowl of chili, she walked in the huge bay doors where I could see some of the guys were washing the truck. A few minutes later, she came back out escorted by an older fireman. I could tell she was upset. He waved as she drove away, and I turned around and headed to the apartment to wait for her to come home. My plan was in motion, and I silently thanked Alex for making this so easy for me.

Arriving back at the apartment, I sprinted upstairs, grabbed Tiny for a quick trip outside then dashed back up to throw myself casually on the futon as if I'd never left. I was anxious to find out what she'd discovered but was willing to wait patiently until she came home to tell me, and I could be there to pick up the pieces and console her.

After a couple of hours, I became concerned. I called Kendall to ask if she'd seen her, and she hadn't so I texted Averi. No reply. Waiting for her to get home was agony, and I watched the clock with great anticipation. Finally, I got a text.

at the pelican. I'll be latte coming homer please take tiny out got peepee. Night.

I jumped up and grabbed my keys. The message was totally crazy but strangely enough, I understood it. The Pelican wasn't far from our place, and I sped over there as fast as I could. Her Jeep was parked out front, and as soon as I got out, I noticed her keys hanging from the ignition. I grabbed them and threw them in my pocket to prevent a possible drunken escape. As soon as I walked in, I could hear loud off-key singing and knew who it was right away.

It was Karaoke night, and Averi was up on the stage belting out 'Before He Cheats' along with Carrie Underwood and actually getting most of the words right. She had a crowd gathered in front of the stage shouting and clapping, and it only spurred her on. Needing no microphone because she had volume all on her own, she had a bottle of tequila in one hand and a shot glass in the other. Foregoing the glass, she tipped the bottle to her lips as the background singers did their thing, spilling some down her shirt, then jumped right back in with Carrie. I could hear the women in the crowd yelling "Amen, sista!" and "Cheatin' ass!" and she'd nod as if in slow motion, pointing at each one. She attempted a high five with one of the waitresses but ended up missing completely causing her to lose her balance for a moment. She held her hands up to let everyone know she was okay then finished her song.

As the applause rang out she picked up the microphone and it squealed with feedback. "Thank you...thank you. Is this on? Testing, testing...hey, I appreciate you clapping for me because I know I suck!" she laughed finishing it out with a snort. "Anyway, I want to tell you all that my ex-boyfriend is a liar and a cheat, in case you didn't get that from my dedication. AND, I caught him tonight! Ladies, stay away from Alex Reynolds...he's a cheating bastard! And to top it off, the bitch is married! Can you believe that?"

There were murmurs from the crowd and one guy shook his fist in the air. "I'll kick his ass for you, sweet thing!" Several more guys stepped forward nodding their heads. I figured I'd better stake a claim before one of the cavemen threw her over his shoulder and made a run for it.

I pushed my way through the crowd until I was in front of her. She looked down at me and gave me a lopsided smile. "Ian, I dreamed about you last night," she slurred. "You were in bed with me and I liked it!" A few of the ladies whistled, and I heard the words 'hot' and 'in my bed anytime' being tossed around. I reached up to take the bottle from her hand, but she wouldn't let go. "Do you know how much I like you?" she asked with a pout. "I love you a whole lot."

I smiled and stepped up onto the stage with her. "Baby, I--" She silenced me with a deep, passionate kiss. There were approving whistles as well as a couple of boos from the cavemen, but I didn't care. I wrapped my arm around her waist and felt her sag against me. I barely caught the bottle as it dropped from her hand and as I set it on the floor, I realized she wasn't standing anymore. Amid cheers, I got her to her feet and started walking her out to the truck, and I heard her mumble, "Ian, I want to find out about my dad but I'm scared."

I managed to get her to the truck, boosted her onto the seat, and after a couple of attempts to snap her seatbelt, I got her safely buckled in. I went around to my side, climbed in and turned the key then saw her lay her head back on the headrest. "I think I'm gonna be sick," she moaned. "I don't wanna but I think I'm gonna."

I reached behind her seat and found an old bucket I'd used for fishing and stuck it on the floor in front of her. "Go for it, if you have to," I said backing out of the parking lot. "Just try to keep it in the bucket."

As we drove in silence with only the occasional hiccup, I thought about what she'd said in the bar. She thought the night she'd asked me to stay had been a dream. All this time, I was worried about her being embarrassed about it, and she hadn't even realized it was real! The sound of snoring got my attention, and I could see she was slumped against the door, her face pressed against the window. As I pulled into our parking lot, she stirred but then faded away again so I gently unbuckled her seatbelt and lifted her into my arms. Once again, she wrapped her arms tightly around me and buried her nose against my neck. "You smell…good," she mumbled. "I love your futon."

Puzzled by her obvious ramblings, I carried her up the stairs and carefully unlocked the door. Since I'd left in such a hurry, I'd forgotten to put Tiny in his crate and he was under my feet as I maneuvered to the bedroom where I carefully placed her on the bed. As I slid off her shoes, I admired her brightly painted pink toes and her tiny toe ring. I stepped back to admire her beauty. Her silky, black hair highlighted with her signature purple and pink streaks was fanned out over the pillow framing her flushed face. Her lips were slightly parted. Her eyes were tightly closed, and I soaked in every last detail. I gently brushed the hair from her face, and her hand shot up to clasp mine. "Ian, I don't want to be alone." Her words trailed off.

Turning off the light, I lay down facing her. "Averi," I whispered, "I need to tell you, this isn't a dream."

The room was dimly lit from the moonlight, and I could see she was studying me. "I know...I don't want you to go." She paused and sighed then the next sound I heard was her gentle snoring.

A few hours passed, and I hadn't slept a wink. I enjoyed listening to her breathing and soft moans as she slept. Then suddenly, she stirred and whispered, "Ian, are you awake?"

"Yes." I said softly.

She sighed. "I guess you heard that Alex cheated on me."

I chuckled softly. "I kinda got that from you yelling it out loud to the entire bar."

She threw her hand over her face. "Oh gosh, I did, didn't I? Well, I guess it's better that I find out now than find out later." She sniffled. "Ian it was horrible. I went to take him the chili like you suggested," she began. "When I got to the station, he wasn't there and when I told them I was his girlfriend, some of the guys started laughing at me. I was humiliated and started to leave but one of the older guys pulled me aside and told me that I seemed like a nice girl and didn't deserve to be treated badly. He told me that he didn't approve of the young guys running around on the young girls and wanted to make sure I didn't get hurt." I nodded just listening. "I'd never been to Alex's place so he gave me his address. Once I found it, his truck was parked there so I walked up to the door and knocked."

She scooted closer to me so I gathered her in my arms. I could feel her trembling so I held her tightly. "Ian, when he came to the door, he was only wearing a towel. His hair was wet like he'd just had a shower. Honestly, he looked shocked to see me, and then I saw why. Some woman came up behind him wrapped in a tiny towel looking at me like 'who in the hell are you?' I was speechless for a moment then I asked if I'd interrupted anything, and before she could say anything, Alex stepped on the deck shutting the door. He told me she was an old friend and that her shower was broken so she'd come over to take one there. He begged me to come back here so we could talk. I could tell she was trying to pull the door open, but he held the knob and told me to go, and he'd be right behind me. I was numb. I didn't know what to do, what to think. I climbed in my Jeep, but I couldn't drive. My hands were shaking, and I wanted to cry. I heard yelling and saw her coming toward me wearing one of Alex's t-shirts and shorts. Alex was chasing behind, trying to stop her, but she pulled away and ran over to me. She looked at me with her hands on her hips and demanded to know who I was. I looked at her dead in the eye and said, 'I was supposed to be his girlfriend! Who in the hell are you?' Alex stepped between us trying to diffuse the situation, but it hit the fan when she glared at me and said, 'Oh yeah, well not tonight!' She was waving her hands in my face, and something caught my eye. She was wearing a big fat wedding band, and I didn't hesitate to mention that. When I did, her whole attitude changed, she turned pale and backed away." Averi took a deep breath. "Alex tried to talk to me but I looked at the both of them and told them they deserved each other then I drove away." She turned her head slightly, and I felt a tear drop on my arm that was cradling her, as she continued. "I drove around for a while then ended up at the Pelican. I knew better than to let it get to me but I've got so much on my mind right now, I needed to let off some steam."

I brushed her hair from her neck and gently placed a kiss against her soft skin. "I totally understand and I also feel really bad because I'm sure I've behaved in the past the same way he did. I've juggled girlfriends and never thought anything of it. You're the reason I changed my ways, Averi. I want to be deserving of someone as beautiful as you."

She sighed. "Ian, I'm sorry but I just don't know what to believe right now…about a lot of things."

Suddenly, her comment about her dad came to mind. "Averi, what did you mean about finding out about your dad." I felt her stiffen so I added, "I'm sorry, I didn't mean to pry."

She shook her head slightly. "No, you're not prying, I brought it up. Truth is, I got a letter from someone claiming to be my biological dad and I just don't know how to deal with it." I rubbed her back gently, and she slowly relaxed against me. "Ian, it's all so confusing. The other day, I went to work and found a letter under my door. It was from someone named Gordon who said he'd known my mom years ago and he suspected he was my real father but that she'd told him he wasn't. He'd been in my shop a couple of days before with his daughter and honestly, she looked a lot like me and our eyes were exactly the same color! After reading his letter, I'm curious. And I also want to know why my mom never told me there could have been someone else. I'm so confused. I called my mom right after I got it but she hasn't called me back."

I thought for a moment then said, "Averi, you have to weigh up the pros and cons. Meeting this guy could turn out to be the best thing that ever happened to you but also could be the worst. You love your dad, or at least the dad you've always known. You don't have any memories of anyone else so in essence, you'd be meeting a stranger. However, if you feel you need to satisfy your curiosity, then call him. If he is your real dad then that also means you have a half-sister and you may want to eventually have a relationship with her."

She looked up at me. "What would you do, Ian? I need advice. I was going to ask Kendall but she's been so busy and on top of that, she's been sick."

Placing my hand under her chin, I looked into her eyes and said, "Follow your heart." Our faces were only inches apart, and I could feel her breath on mine.

So softly I could hardly hear her, she said, "Kiss me."

I sighed. "I don't want you to do anything you'd regret tomorrow. I want to kiss you, more than you could ever imagine. I want to be with you, make love to you...but I don't want it to be for the wrong reasons."

She gently ran her fingers through my hair. "Ian, I might've had some tequila tonight but I was fully aware of everything that happened. When I kissed you at the bar, I knew right then, it wasn't enough. And for your information, I wanted you long before tonight. And this isn't about Alex...he's never had my heart." She gently pressed her lips to mine. "I need you in more ways than you know."

My heart was hammering in my chest at the words I'd longed to hear. "Are you sure, baby?" I asked as I cupped her cheek. "Because I want this more than anything."

Her answer was to wrap her fingers in my hair and again draw my mouth to hers. The sweetness of her lips was intoxicating, and I found myself lost in the sensation. My hands wrapped around her, finding the bare flesh I was so desperate to touch. She tugged at my shirt and with my help, in one motion, she slipped it off and tossed it into the darkness. Her hands feathered up my bare chest to stop right above my heart.

"Your heart is pounding," she whispered. She rubbed her cheek across my skin then turned to touch her lips to the spot where my heart was now racing.

I swallowed hard. "It's because of you," I managed to choke out. Our eyes met, and she kissed me again. Our lips joined softly at first, with just tentative brushes, but then I felt her tongue slide over my bottom lip, and I gasped as I met her tongue with mine. I could feel all the tension she'd been feeling drift away as my hands stroked her bare skin. Sliding my hands into her hair, I deepened the kiss and moaned against her mouth as she raked her nails softly down my back. Rolling her onto her back, I shifted my body to cover hers partly. She wrapped her leg around mine, sliding her foot up and down my calf. The anticipation of being together was almost more than I could stand. I broke the kiss to look into her eyes. "Averi, you're everything I've ever wanted and needed in my life."

I saw tears well in her eyes. "Ian, don't play games with my heart. It's yours, please just don't break it." Wiping the tear that escaped from her eye, I nodded slowly then tenderly kissed her, my hands pulling off her t-shirt to reveal the lacy black bra I'd seen hanging on the shower rod. Taking my fingertips, I traced the edge of the strap down to slide around to unhook her bra. I could hardly breathe as, without taking her eyes from mine, she reached up and slid the straps down then pulled it completely off tossing it in the direction of my shirt. My hands wandered over her silky soft skin, and I felt her arch her back, her breath coming in short bursts. I captured her mouth again in a slow deep kiss.

Her hands found my chest again then slid down my stomach, my muscles jerking at her touch. Her eyes met mine and locked on as she unbuttoned my pants, but I put my hand on hers to stop us from going any further without taking precautions. "I'll be right back," I whispered.

"It's okay," she said softly.

"Averi, I've always used protection. Are you sure?" I asked.

"I'm clean and I'm on the pill. I've never gone without either, but I trust you Ian and I want to feel all of you," she whispered.

I took a deep breath. She held out her hand to me, and I knelt beside her on the bed. "You are spectacular," I said as I kissed each fingertip then her palm, and she closed her eyes and sighed. My eyes swept over her perfectly toned body, and I felt almost drunk with desire. Her tiny black panties hugged her hips, the lacy material leaving nothing to the imagination. I lay beside her and began tracing my fingers up her taut abdomen delighting in every sigh and moan she made.

Her beautiful brown eyes opened, and she smiled leaving me breathless. I nuzzled her neck breathing in the familiar scent of her shampoo then ran my tongue lightly over her earlobe. She shivered in my arms in response then arched her back as if greedy for more. I could tell she was getting impatient, but I wanted this to be unrushed. We were in this moment in time, and I was going to cherish every second of it. I whispered, "Easy, baby. We'll get there."

I tucked my fingers under the delicate lace of her panties and slid them down inch by inch until they dangled on her toes. With a flip of her foot, they disappeared. "Now, it's your turn," she purred. Her hands again found the buttons of my jeans and instead of carefully unbuttoning each one, she pulled until each button popped open. She looked up and with a coy smile said, "I'm sorry, I guess I don't know my own strength." Jeans were not designed to slip off easily so I just backed off the bed and let them drop. She giggled and for a moment, I was a little offended then I looked down and realized I had my Big Headed boxers on. "A little conceited, are we?" She said still giggling.

I shrugged giving her a lopsided grin. "Hey, what can I say? And they're wicked comfortable." Dropping the boxers in a heap beside my jeans, I joined her on the bed. Her giggles were gone now, replaced by a seductive come-hither look. My body was taut with anticipation, and I captured her lips, grasping her waist with my hands to pull her to me. "This is so right," I murmured. Covering her body with mine, I searched her eyes for any sign of doubt but there was none. As we joined, she gasped and held me tightly. Our mouths found each other again and slowly our bodies found their rhythm, and the only sound was our breathing. I felt her hands tighten on my back and saw her eyes flutter as a moan escaped her slightly parted lips. It was almost more than I could handle, the sensations more intense than I'd ever experienced before. Our eyes locked as we rode the waves of desire until we shattered, hearts thudding against each other's chests. I couldn't speak. My head dropped to the pillow beside hers, and I feathered kisses along her jaw. As she turned her head, I saw a huge smile on her face.

"That was freakin' incredible," she gasped. I gave her a huge smile in return. We lay there trying to catch our breath, our limbs tangled together in the sheets. After a few minutes, we'd recovered enough to move and nuzzling her ear, I suggested we take a shower.

"I'll get the water started," she said getting up to head to the bathroom. It was then I saw the tattoo. "Damn woman, that henna is sexy as hell."

She grinned. "Rochelle did it." As she walked from the room, I blew out a whistle.

"Now I know where the phrase 'Do you want some fries with that shake?' comes from!" I said with a grin. She glanced over her shoulder and gave me one more wiggle as she walked in to start the shower. The steam was billowing from the door as I walked in. I could see her outline behind the curtain, and I flashed back to that first time I'd interrupted her shower. I'd tried to be as calm as possible that day while holding a razor right next to my face. This time, I was welcome to join her, and as I slid back the curtain, she beckoned me with a sexy smile.

Chapter 11

Averi

I had a feeling of déjà vu as he climbed into the tub with me and flushed as I realized this was my fantasy come to life. The water cascaded down his muscular torso as he stood under the spray. He squirted some shampoo in his hand and began to wash my hair, his fingers slowly massaging my scalp as he looked down into my eyes. I closed my eyes enjoying his hands working the suds through my hair. He turned me around and backed me into the stream of water to rinse the shampoo from my hair then spun me around to kiss me. He leaned in close and sniffed my hair. "You smell amazing, baby," he growled. He picked up my loofah, which he then loaded with body wash. He began to wash my skin in slow, circular motions, and I could feel my breaths becoming shorter as my heart began to beat faster. He trailed the loofah down my neck then followed it with tiny kisses, which tickled, but at the same time, were hot as hell. "Let me see you," he whispered as he pushed me back slightly. His eyes roamed up and down my body, and I felt my face flush with desire. "Now, your back. I really want to study this tattoo," he growled. He kissed my shoulder then trailed his kisses all the way down to my hip. "Baby, this is hot," he murmured against my skin.

As he stood to kiss me, I pulled the loofah from his hand. Huskily, I said, "Now it's your turn."

I bathed him giving him the same attention, he'd given me. He kept interrupting me with kisses which I didn't mind at all. The water finally cooled, and we were forced to leave the shower. We climbed out, gently toweled each other off, and he whispered, "Now that I've seen your lacy unmentionables, next, I want to see that mysterious toy box."

Blushing, I grinned and nodded. "Soon, very soon."

Dressing quickly, I realized we'd forgotten all about Tiny but when we went out into the living room, he was fast asleep on the futon with a half-eaten remote control hanging halfway out of his slack mouth. Ian looked at me sideways and said, "So, does this mean he's sleeping out here from now on?"

"Hmm, I guess you can share with him." I started to walk away and felt myself being lifted in the air and spun around.

"You think you're funny?" he said before giving me a kiss. "He's really cute but I think you're cuter."

He pressed his forehead to mine, and I gave him a quick kiss. "Okay, you talked me into it. You can share with me," I laughed.

He beamed. "It would be my pleasure. So, do you need to get ready for work?"

I grinned. "Actually, no. Rochelle is working for me today. I actually get to have a couple of days off!"

"Whoo hoo!" he said as he spun me around again. Tiny woke up and started jumping and barking while trying to grab my foot as it went by. We were laughing so hard that we almost didn't hear Ian's phone ring. He set me down, gave me another kiss and grabbed his phone. "It's Tristan," he said before answering. "Hey, what's up?" He asked.

I couldn't hear what Tristan was saying but Ian's face fell. "Where are you taking her?" he asked with concern. He turned his back to me as he got a response then Ian said, "Yeah, she's here with me. We'll head over there now."

He hung up the phone then turned to face me. "Tristan's taking Kendall to the hospital."

"What's wrong?" I asked grabbing Tiny to run him outside for a pit stop.

He grabbed his keys and followed me down the steps. "Tristan said she fainted while she was making breakfast. When she fell, she got a pretty deep gash on her head. He's got her in the car and they're on the way to the ER now. I'll pull the car around while you put Tiny back in the apartment and meet you in the parking lot."

After leaving Tiny securely in his crate, I dashed down the steps and into the waiting car. We arrived at the hospital and quickly located Tristan, who was pacing the waiting room.

"Tristan, is she okay?" I asked walking up behind him.

He spun around when he heard me and shrugged. "I have no idea. They took her right back because she was bleeding heavily, so heavily it soaked right through the towel we used to try to stop the flow. The nurse who took her back told me to wait out here."

I felt a little faint myself at the thought of her losing blood, so I clutched Ian's arm for support. He put his arm around me and led me to an empty chair. "Here, sit down and I'll get you some water." Taking deep, even breaths, I was able to shake the light-headed feeling but was still grateful for the cold bottle of water Ian brought to me.

Tristan sat down on one side of me and Ian on the other. "So, tell us what happened exactly," Ian said as he gently rubbed his hand on my back to soothe me.

"Well, she had a doctor's appointment a couple of days ago because she'd been feeling run down and exhausted and thought she was getting the flu. She'd go from blazing hot one minute to freezing cold the next. She felt so bad, she'd been barely eating and I really think that's why she fainted. She's let herself get run down and then when she tried to surprise me with breakfast in bed, she ends up in the hospital."

I was confused. "So, what happened at the doctor's appointment? Did they do any tests?" I asked.

Tristan shook his head. "She never got to the appointment because she overslept and missed it. The office called and woke her up but by then they couldn't fit her in. They rescheduled for tomorrow but hopefully we'll find out something while we're here."

"Gosh, that doesn't sound like Kendall at all." I began to get a knot in my stomach thinking something serious could be going on when a nurse came out to get Tristan.

"Mr. O'Neal?" she asked. When he nodded, she took him by the arm and walked him back to the triage area.

"Averi, she's going to be fine," Ian said pulling me to him to rest my head on his shoulder. "A few stitches and she'll be as good as new."

A few minutes later, Tristan came back out with a smile. "She's doing much better. They've stitched her up and are giving her an IV for dehydration. When she found out you both were here, she yelled at me for worrying you."

I laughed. "Now that sounds more like Kendall. Are they going to be keeping her much longer?"

Tristan nodded. "Yeah, they're keeping her for observation since she hit her head pretty hard and are doing a few tests to try to figure out why she's so run down. Those results should be back in a few minutes. In the meantime, we can go back to her room and sit with her, if you want."

We made our way through the triage into the actual emergency room. Every room was occupied which explained why the waiting area was so full. I was so thankful that Kendall had been taken care of so quickly but also said a little prayer for those who were waiting. We walked into her curtained room as the nurse was attaching another bag of fluid to her IV. Kendall was laying on a hospital bed with her eyes closed but they fluttered open as we came in. "Hey guys," she said groggily. "Sorry to make you worry."

I rushed over to take her hand. "Sorry? You have nothing to be sorry for. We're just glad you're okay!" I took in the large square gauze bandage on her forehead. "You really did a number on your head, huh?"

Tristan leaned over to kiss her cheek. "How're you feeling, babe?" Worry creased his forehead.

She gave him a weak smile. "I'm doing better now that you're here." She clutched his hand and held it to her cheek. Turning to me, she rolled her eyes. "Yeah, when I do it, I do it right."

The sound of the curtain being whisked back got our attention. A man sporting a stethoscope came in carrying a chart. "Good morning, Mrs. O'Neal. I'm Dr. Fletcher." Tristan and I stepped away to let him carry out his exam. He held a penlight in front of her pupils and flashed it side to side. "Looks good," he said smiling. "I think you'll be ready to go home in another hour or so. In the meantime, I need to talk to you about how you've been feeling lately." He glanced over at us and said, "This is your private health information…"

"They can stay," Kendall interrupted. "They're family."

The doctor shrugged and smiled. "Works for me. Now, we got the test results back and everything looks okay. They gave us a good idea as to why you've been feeling so weak and tired. As it turns out, you're pregnant. You'll need to do some further tests with an OB--"

"Pregnant!?" Tristan and Kendall asked in unison.

He smiled. "Yes, it's very early in the pregnancy but the blood tests confirmed it." He made another note in the chart then said, "I'll let you absorb the news and be back shortly to start your discharge paperwork."

As soon as he cleared the curtain, Tristan said with a smile, "That explains a lot." Kendall's mouth flapped but no words came out. Taking her hand, he said, "We're having a baby…this is amazing."

I rushed back over to Kendall's bedside to give her hand a squeeze. "This is so wonderful. I'm so happy for you!"

She seemed a bit dazed but slowly a smile spread across her face.

"A baby!" she said laughing nervously. "And I thought it was just the flu!" Tristan brushed his hand against her cheek. "I'm really happy," she said swallowing hard. "Nauseous, but happy."

I got up and walked over to Ian. "Hey, why don't you buy me a cup of coffee?" I took his arm and led him from the room. When we were out of earshot, I said, "I think they need some alone time to digest the news. Don't you think?"

He smiled and nodded. "I want some alone time, too…with you." He backed me against the wall bracing his arms on either side of me. "I can't stop thinking about--"

"Ian?" I heard a female voice come from behind him. "Is that you? I haven't seen you since that night you took me home from the Rascal Flatts concert."

Ian turned around tucking me behind him. "Well, hey. How've you been?" He asked casually.

He was blocking my view, so I poked him hard in the ribs. "Ouch!" he yelled. As he moved, I could finally see who he was talking to. It was Amanda Childers, who had been a classmate of ours and was now, by her appearance, a nurse at this hospital.

Her eyes grew wide with surprise. "Well, hey there, Averi," she said through a strained smile. "What are you doing hiding back there?" We'd never been friends in school and it looked as if we weren't going to start now.

"Oh nothing really. Just waiting for my friend to get discharged." I looked up at Ian and gave him a sweet smile. "I'll go get my own coffee. You visit with your bunny." He flinched and I could tell I'd hit a nerve, but it also irked me that we couldn't go anywhere without running into one of his former flames.

I left them standing there and didn't look back. I found the vending machines, got my coffee and headed back to Kendall's room. When I arrived, Tristan was on his way out. "Averi, good…can you sit with Kendall for a few minutes? I have to call work and let them know what's going on. The reception in this place sucks!"

"Sure, knock yourself out." He punched me lightly on the shoulder and headed out the door.

Cradling my coffee in my hands, I sat down next to Kendall's bed. She was laying there with a blissful smile on her face, so I could only imagine their talk had given her some peace of mind. "Averi, I have the best husband! He's going to be a great dad."

I smiled and nodded. "He really is a great guy. You are so perfect together and you'll be great parents." As I said the word parents, I thought of mine and quickly checked my phone. I'd missed a call from my mom so I checked to see if there was a voicemail, but there wasn't one. I silently cursed missing her call. I still needed to talk to her about Gordon. "Speaking of parents, I have some news."

She sat up a little to get a sip of water. "What's up? Are they okay?"

I took a deep breath. "Yeah, they're good, I guess. I haven't talked to them in a few days. That's not what I want to tell you." I paused then just blurted it out. "My dad may not be my real dad."

She almost spit her water across the room. "What are you saying?" She gasped.

I got her a tissue from the nightstand to mop up the spray then sat back down. "I got a letter from someone claiming to be my real dad." I proceeded to tell her what the letter said and her eyes got bigger and bigger.

"Oh gosh, Averi! Do you think it could be possible?" I then told her about Brianna's unusual eyes and how similar we were. As I said it out loud to her it seemed more plausible than ever. "What are you going to do?"

Shrugging, I said, "I don't really know. I really want to talk to my mom and see what she has to say. I only have a few more days to contact him before he goes back to Nashville. He said if I didn't call him by then, he'd never bother me again."

She held her hand out to me, and I scooted my chair closer to take it. "I'm sorry you've had to deal with this on your own. I've been dealing with my sick self and neglected you."

"Um, I can take a backseat to your baby any day! I can tell you all my crazy news when you're feeling better."

Kendall scooted up in her bed and glared. "There's more? Excuse me? You know I have to know what's going on with you."

I sighed. "Okay, if you insist. I caught Alex cheating on me with some married woman, went to the Pelican to perform drunk Karaoke and ended up in bed with Ian." I groaned as the scene from the hallway flashed through my head. "Kendall, it happened. Now, I'm not so sure that was a good thing. Ian's got a past and it seems to find us wherever we go. I don't regret what happened, I just don't know if he's a one woman kinda guy."

She nodded slowly. "Did you sleep with him as a revenge thing?" She asked forcing me to look at her.

I threw my hand over my face. "I don't know. I'm all screwed up in the head right now. Too much is happening all at once. I feel like I'm stuck in a bad soap opera."

Kendall pulled my hand from my face. "Well, this is one of those times when you need to put your big girl panties on and take care of each thing in its own way. From the sound of it, you took care of the Alex situation. You're a strong woman, Averi, even though it doesn't feel like it. You have two more very important things to deal with and the only way to do it is head-on."

She was right. I really needed to take care of this on my own without whining and waiting for someone to fix it for me. "Okay, you win. I'll call Gordon later today and meet with him." I paused. "As for Ian, I just don't know what to do. He's so sweet when he's alone with me but when we're out in public, we always seem to run into someone he has some sort of past with…"

The sound of the curtain being pulled back stopped me cold. It was Tristan. "You ready to make your escape?" he asked as he rolled a wheelchair into the room. "Ian's gone to get the truck so I can carry you away," he said as he helped her sit up. Once she was safely in the chair, he gathered her things and seeing his hands were full, I offered to carry them. As he rolled her out the automatic doors, Ian stopped the truck directly in front of us. I opened the door to place her things inside and backed away to let her get in. She gingerly climbed in and after Tristan made sure she was safely buckled in, she lay her head back against the seat.

"Call me later," I called out right before Tristan shut her door. He then jogged around to the driver's side, hopped in and they headed to their house.

Chapter 12

Ian

"Well, let's go. Tiny probably needs to go out," I said brusquely as I walked to my truck. I opened her door then shut it firmly behind her. Without a word, I climbed in, cranked it and pulled out onto the road.

We rode in silence for a few minutes, then finally she said, "So, how *is* Amanda?" I didn't respond so she kept talking. "I bet she's ready for Rascal Flatts to come back to town so she can get a repeat performance."

I took a deep breath trying to keep my voice even. "Yeah, she and her fiancé, Erik, have already gotten their tickets. They're taking their little boy, Jacob, with them this time. The last time she saw them in concert, she was seven months pregnant with him and Erik was deployed to Afghanistan." Out of the corner of my eye, I saw her face begin to flush as I continued, "I was working security at the concert and happened to run into her. She'd been standing for most of the concert so I rented her a chair to make her more comfortable. The girls she'd ridden with all got trashed and decided to spend the night in a nearby hotel but she'd started feeling some pre-labor pains, so she wanted to go back home. I gave her a ride and that was the last time I saw her until today. Her fiancé is home for good now and they're planning a wedding in a few months."

She squirmed in her seat keeping her gaze out the window. "That was a great thing you did," she said softly.

"Yeah, Averi. I'm not such a low-life. I've been trying to prove that to you but every time some girl walks up to me, you assume she was one of my—what did you call them again? Bunnies?"

She slunk further down into her seat. "Ian, I'm sorry. I shouldn't have assumed--"

"It's okay, Averi. I wouldn't trust me either." The conversation ended as we pulled into the parking lot.

After I parked, I turned off the truck, and we just sat there. The silence was deafening. "Well, I guess I'll go check on Tiny," she whispered as she opened her door. I should have stopped her, but I didn't move.

"Yeah," I said looking away. "Go check on him. I'm gonna drive around for a while." Alone with my thoughts,

I replayed the conversation that ripped me to shreds. I'd
been seconds from pulling back the curtain of Kendall's
hospital room when I heard them talking about me.
Hearing her say she didn't know about me, didn't know if
she could deal with my past, was like a knife to my gut.
The shame of my past and my obvious inability to prove
my feelings to her made me want to kick myself in the ass.
I'd been so foolish all my life never thinking that the
skeletons in my closet would come prancing out to ruin my
chance at true happiness.

It was several hours before I eventually got back and when
I walked into the apartment, she was gone and my first
thought was that she'd taken Tiny for a walk. After an
hour, I called her phone, which went straight to voicemail.
Worried, I'd also tried Tristan and Kendall's phones but
nobody was answering. Several hours later, I finally got
Kendall. It turned out, as soon as they'd gotten home from
the hospital, they'd turned off their phones to be able to get
some sleep. When I explained why I was calling, I could
tell Kendall was getting upset, something a pregnant lady
with a bump on her head didn't need to be. Tristan took the
phone. "What's going on?" He asked.

I blurted out, "Have you heard anything from Averi? I'm worried sick! I came home and she's gone, the dog's gone…"

"Ian, slow down. Did you call her phone?"

"Of course I did! She's not answering and it goes straight to voicemail. Her Jeep's in the parking lot and her stuff is still here." I stepped on one of Tiny's toys and cursed as it bit into my foot.

"What the heck?" Tristan asked.

"Damnit, I stepped on a toy. Anyway, I was a total ass earlier and I--" I hesitated then said, "Well, I said some things--" Again I paused. "Yeah…I'm this close to calling the police."

I was pacing back and forth when I heard the door open. Averi walked in carrying Tiny. Relief flooded over me. "Hey, she's here. Let me call you back." I hung up the phone and tossed it onto the futon. Seeing her safe and sound in front of me, nothing mattered except wrapping her in my arms and never letting go. "I was so worried!" I said, my lips against her hair. "I thought something had happened to you."

"Ian?" she mumbled. "You're squishing me." I relaxed my grip but still didn't let her go. Finally, she said, "Um, Tiny needs some space and besides that, he's heavy." She groaned.

That got my attention and I let her go and took Tiny from her arms. I put him down on the floor, tossed him the squeaky toy I'd stepped on earlier then turned my attention back to her.

"So, where've you been? Honestly, I've been crazy since I came home and found you weren't here." I took her by the arms, pulled her close and kissed her forehead. "I'm so sorry about earlier. I shouldn't have acted like I did. Can you forgive me?"

"Ian, first of all, I was the one who started everything by accusing you of being with Amanda. It was immature and stupid…just like letting my phone die. And secondly…I went to meet Gordon." I was confused for a moment then I realized who she was talking about.

"You met with him? Alone? Do you know how dangerous that was?"

She nodded. "Yes, and I'm a big girl. I met him in a public place and took my bodyguard along." We both looked down at Tiny who was now on his back biting his own front paw. "After you dropped me off, I realized how stupid I'd been acting. I've been so mixed up with everything going on in my life and the only person to fix it was me. I started with Gordon."

She pulled away from me and started pacing. I sat down to let her have room. "When he answered, at first I didn't know what to say. Finally, I managed a hello. He knew who I was right away. I told him how nervous I was and instead of laughing at me, which I expected, he told me he knew how I felt and that he was hoping I'd call. That made things a little easier. Before I chickened out, I asked if he'd like to meet somewhere to talk and he sounded so pleased. He asked me when and where so I used my brains and thought of a public place where I'd be safe…Britt's Donuts. I realized I didn't want to lock Tiny up again so I decided to take him with me. Since it's so close, we walked. When I rounded the corner to Britt's, I saw him waving with a big smile on his face. The first thing I noticed were his eyes…they were exactly like mine and I tried not to stare. We got some donuts, then we wandered down to the marina where all of the party boats are. They were filling up with the passengers for the sightseeing cruises. Honestly, it was awkward at first but then he finally broke the ice. We started comparing our likes and dislikes, hands, feet...turns out we have the same weird toe." She looked down at her foot as she wiggled her toes with a wistful smile. "Anyway, after a while, I realized, it wasn't about physical characteristics so much as I could feel a connection to him. It was a strange feeling and I really didn't want to admit it to him right away. Finally, I was the one who brought up the paternity test."

She stopped pacing. "Ian, I want to know, for sure. I've thought about this and I don't want my mom or dad to know about the test until afterwards. I've tried calling her and we've missed each other each time so I'm taking that as a sign."

"I understand," I said leaning forward to take her hand.

She wrapped her fingers around mine. "He said he really loved her. I get the feeling he's telling me the truth."

She sighed and sat down next to me still holding my hand. "He leaves in a few days so we're going to find a lab to do a DNA test. He'll be going back to Tennessee before the results come back but he promised he'd come back to find out with me. He hasn't told his family any of this. He figures that conversation will come in due time, if it's necessary." I put my arm around her shoulder and pulled her close. "Ian, I'm scared. If this test proves he's my dad…well, everything's going to change."

"Averi, it doesn't have to. The man you've always called Dad is, and always will be, your dad. You won't love him any less. It doesn't just go away."

She nodded. "You're right and thank you for being here for me."

I lifted her hand to my lips. "And I always will be. I just want to make sure you don't get hurt."

She smiled. "I appreciate that, I really do. I think this is something I have to do." Her eyes locked onto mine. "And this is something else I have to do." She stood pulling me to my feet. She slid her hand up to pull my face down to hers. She stood on her toes to press her sweet lips to mine, and I easily lifted her up to eye level. Our kiss was slow and deliberate, and I moaned with desire as she wrapped her legs around my waist to keep us together. "Ian, take me to bed…" Her words trailed away seductively.

I kissed her and said, "…or I'll lose you forever? Well, I don't want that to happen so to the bedroom we go." And we did. It was an unexpected pleasure to have her take control and when we made love, she had an abandon that took my breath away.

Now, as I lay beside her watching her sleep, it hit me how much I really loved her. I could feel a connection to her and it was so strong like a magnetic force pulling us together. My only wish was that she felt the same way.

Listening to her steady breathing, her warm skin against mine, I cherished just having her close. She was mine, for now, and I was going to make every moment count. Finally, I closed my eyes, snuggled into her and drifted off to sleep.

When I woke up, I immediately noticed she wasn't next to me. I heard clattering outside the bedroom door, so I got out of bed and threw on some shorts. When I walked into the kitchen, the sight that met my eyes was mind-blowingly sexy. She was standing in the kitchen in just a tiny bikini. Her hair pulled up in her usual messy bun. Tiny was sprawled on the futon with one of my sneakers tucked under his head. When he saw me, he barked and Averi turned giving me a huge smile. "Good morning, sleepyhead," she said standing on her toes to give me a kiss. "I'm making breakfast."

I feigned shock. "You cooked!?" I clutched my chest and backed into the table.

She rolled her eyes, and I could tell she was fighting the urge to smile. "Very funny. I'm sure Tiny will be glad to eat yours." She put a plate of freshly cooked bacon and sausage next to a plate stacked with pancakes. "The scrambled eggs are almost ready." As she finished cooking, I poured some coffee and set both cups on the table then took a seat. She brought the steaming eggs to the table and was about to sit, but I jumped up to pull her chair out for her. "Well, aren't you a gentleman this morning."

I nuzzled her neck then kissed her shoulder. "I had ulterior motives," I growled. I got the desired result when she shivered. "Are we staying in today?" I whispered.

She gave me a sexy smile then laughed. "Well, not *all* day! It's Sunday, I don't have to work and I want to go to the beach. It's perfect weather and I want to work on my tan."

"Okay, we'll go to the beach but only if I get to rub lotion on you," I said with a mischievous grin.

She grinned. "It's a deal."

We finished breakfast and after I ran Tiny out for a walk, we headed down to the beach. We carried chairs, an umbrella and a cooler of cold drinks and claimed a spot where we knew the tide wouldn't come to wash us away. I set up our chairs and the umbrella then she moved the cooler under the shade. The lotion was in my hand as soon as she pulled off her oversized t-shirt and I took my job seriously making sure not to miss anywhere. "I think you're enjoying this just a little too much," she said laughing. She returned the favor by rubbing lotion on me, and then we sat side by side in the chairs, our fingers entwined watching the kids play in the surf. A plane flew by pulling a banner behind it and I squinted to see what it was advertising. The banner proclaimed a seafood special at one of the local restaurants. "I wonder how many people see those things," Averi said sheltering her eyes with her hand. "I was thinking of renting one to advertise for the shop."

I shrugged. "A lot is my guess. The plane rides down the beach and back over town. It circles around several times. I have a friend who knows the guy with the plane. I can ask him if you want."

She sat back in her chair and sighed. "Yeah, that'd be great. It's just a thought. Hey, I think I'm going to go let

Tiny have a little stretch. Do you want anything from home? A sandwich?"

I shook my head no. "I'm good." I happily made note of the word 'home'. "Do you want me to come with you?" I started to get up, but she pushed me back by my shoulder.

Looking around at our little oasis she said, "No, that would be silly to pack up everything for just a few minutes. I'll be back in a little bit." She slipped on her t-shirt and flip flops and headed back to the apartment.

I lay my head back and closed my eyes listening to the sounds of the kids splashing around and the conversations of the people in the chairs closest to us. The sun was warm and made me very sleepy. Suddenly, I felt cold water splash across my chest startling me. My eyes popped open to find a bikini clad body directly in front of me blocking the sun, and it wasn't Averi.

"Hey Ian!" a female voice said as I squinted trying to make out who it was. "Don't you remember me? Taylor? We hung out at Hobie's last summer."

She plopped down in Averi's chair without asking and I said, "That chair's taken."

She pouted. "By who? I don't see anyone."

"By me…that's who." Averi was standing behind the chair with her hands on her hips. "Move it!" Taylor turned around obviously surprised and she jumped up, backing away. Averi moved to stand in front of the chair. She gracefully sat down then linked her fingers with mine. "So, you were saying?" she asked with one eyebrow raised. Taylor glared at us both then turned on her heels and left. "I hope you don't mind me taking care of that. If we're going to be seeing each other, for however long it lasts, I want it to just be me."

Lifting her hand to my lips, I said, "Averi, you've got me. I don't want anyone else."

She gave me a sad smile, and I still saw doubt in her eyes. This was going to take time, but I wasn't going anywhere.

We spent the day sitting quietly on the beach and as the day ended, we took our things back to the apartment and decided to take Tiny for a walk. The sand had cooled as the sun went down in the sky. We paddled in the water feeling the tide pulling against our feet. I slung my arm over her shoulder as we walked stealing kisses when I could. Up ahead of us, on his leash, Tiny was chasing a hermit crab but gave up when it dug itself into the sand and disappeared. We wandered back as it grew darker. Once we got home, we curled up with a bowl of popcorn and I made her watch 'Top Gun'. We were halfway through when her phone rang so I paused it as she jumped up to answer it.

"Hey!" she said before mouthing *Gordon*. I couldn't hear his end of the conversation but from Averi's side, he apparently wanted to confirm their meeting to do the paternity test. They agreed on a time, and she got the address to the lab. "I'll see you in the morning," she said before hanging up.

"I couldn't help but overhear. You're meeting tomorrow?" I asked pulling her into my lap.

She nodded. "Yeah, I've got butterflies in my stomach. This is becoming so real." She lay her head on my shoulder. "If he *is* my dad, I've got to figure out what to do next."

I gently kissed her forehead. "If it would make things easier, I could go with you. I'm supposed to go back to work tomorrow but I can call in late." I gently stroked her hair and felt her relax against me.

She raised her head to give me a smile and a gentle kiss. "I appreciate the offer but I think I need to do this on my own.

I may need you to go with me when we get the results, so I'll definitely take a rain check."

Chapter 13

Averi

It was still early when I felt Ian kiss my cheek before climbing out of bed. "I'll call you later to see how it goes," he whispered. I nodded sleepily and promptly fell back to sleep. An hour later, the alarm on my phone chirped me awake. I crawled out of bed and saw Tiny was still fast asleep. I found a note on the kitchen counter.

Took Tiny out so you could sleep later. I'll be thinking of you today.

I called Rochelle to make sure she knew to open and assured her I'd be in by lunchtime. I took a quick shower then looked through my closet for something appropriate to wear. I settled on a vintage lavender sundress that I'd picked up at the consignment shop. I also liked that it matched the purple in my hair. I grabbed a pair of lavender flip flops that were adorned with a big blingy gem. I left my hair loose, put on a dab of lip gloss, and I was out the door.

When I arrived at the lab, I sat in my Jeep for a moment trying to calm myself. My hands were trembling and I had a huge knot in my stomach, but I knew I had to do this, for my own peace of mind.

"Averi!" I heard my name and turned to see Gordon had driven up and was getting out of his rental car. "Perfect timing!" He walked over to open my door. "You look very pretty today," he said smiling.

"Thank you." I grabbed my wallet then climbed down with his help. "I'm a little freaked out about all of this so please forgive me if I seem a little out of it."

We walked into the building and were greeted by the receptionist. Gordon had made an appointment so after we checked in, we sat together in the waiting room. "So, how's your puppy?" Gordon asked in an obvious attempt to make small talk.

I laughed. "He's fine. Eating everything in sight, including Ian's shoe."

"Ian?" He raised an eyebrow. "Is that your boyfriend?"

I hesitated before I answered. "Um, really? I don't know what he is. We're roommates but it's gotten a little more serious lately. I was dating someone else not too long ago but I found out he was cheating on me. Since then, Ian and I have been kinda seeing each other, I guess you could say."

"Well, I'm glad you found out about the cheating part. I don't believe in it and if this test proves I'm really not your father then--"

I bit my lower lip to stop the quivering and swallowed back the huge lump in my throat as I nodded. "We'll just wait and see what happens."

Two technicians came out to get us, and I was taken to one exam room while Gordon was taken to another. I sat down on the paper-covered exam table and watched as the tech prepared the testing kit. She had swabs and plastic vials laid out on a rolling tray beside the table.

"So," she said consulting the paperwork. "You're Averi Rain and you wish to have paternity testing done with…Gordon Haynes?" She looked up, and I nodded.

"Okay, Ms. Rain. I'll need you to open your mouth and I'm going to swab the inside of your cheek firmly." I took a deep breath and let her do her thing and when she was finished, she slid the swab into a plastic vial bearing a label with my name. "We'll do one more for a backup and then we're done," she said grabbing another swab. When we'd finished, I came down the hallway to the waiting area, and I could hear Gordon talking to someone.

"Yes, I'm here to find out if I have a daughter," he said.

A woman's voice said, "Well, if looks have anything to do with it, you didn't need the test. I saw you both when you came in and honestly, I was surprised you were here for that."

Gordon laughed. "I agree completely and I feel she's mine in my gut. I only hope the test doesn't let me down." As I walked into the room, they both looked over at me, and I saw them share a nod and a grin. "Well, it was nice talking to you," he said standing up to walk me to the checkout desk.

"Good luck, you two," was her reply.

After we checked out, Gordon walked me to my Jeep. "Well, it says five days is the turnaround time. I'm going to head home with the family tomorrow and then I'll fly back as soon as we get the results. I told the lab that we didn't want to be notified by phone, only in person. I want to be here when we find out."

"Gordon, I'm scared," I said with a quivering voice. "You're really a nice person but now this is becoming too real for me. I love my dad and I just don't know what this will do to him or my mom, for that matter."

He put his hand on my shoulder and gave it a squeeze. "Averi, I don't want this to change your feelings for your parents. If I'm your dad, I just want to be a part of your life, even if it is just a small one."

That made me feel better. "Thank you. I'm glad you understand." I climbed into my Jeep. "Have a safe trip home and I'll see you soon." I backed out of my space and headed to the shop.

When I arrived, Rochelle was doing an ear piercing on a young woman. "Everything good?" I asked as I walked by to throw my things behind the counter.

"Yup," she said as she carefully pushed the needle through her ear then inserted the earring. "We've had a couple of lookers and one guy said he needed to talk to you so I told him you'd be in after lunch."

I went into the back and slipped off my dress throwing on my work t-shirt and shorts. When I walked out, Rochelle was ringing up the sale. "I want to tell you, that was the first piercing I ever had that didn't hurt," the woman said as she handed the money to her.

"Why, thank you and come again!" Rochelle said with a big smile.

I checked all the supplies and then looked at the time. "Hey, you can take your lunch now. I've got it."

"Thanks, boss!" She said as she dashed out the door.

I was writing up the bank deposit from the day before when I heard the door chime. Glancing up, my heart leapt to my throat. Alex. Crap, crap, crap! I took a deep breath and spoke as coolly as I could. "What can I do for you?"

He looked around to make sure we were alone before speaking. "I need to talk to you. It's really important."

"Alex, I don't believe we have anything to talk about." I turned my back to him indicating he could leave, but instead he grabbed my arm and spun me around to face him.

"Ouch! That hurt!" I squealed.

He relaxed his grip but held on. "Sorry, I would never hurt you, Averi. You know me better than that, right?"

"Really, Alex? At this point, I'm not sure I know you at all." I tried to pull free but he held on. Finally, I said, "What? What is so important?"

He seemed really nervous which kinda freaked me out a little. "Okay, well...here goes. The other day, when you came to my apartment, you totally misjudged what was going on. As you know, Diane, the woman who was at my place is married but I swear to you, nothing was going on. That being said, her husband, who is also a fireman, is threatening divorce because word got back to him that we were together. I need you to go with me to talk to him and tell him that you're my girlfriend and that there's nothing between her and me."

My mouth dropped open. "Are you serious? Alex, I saw you both in practically nothing! You looked like you'd just come out of the shower together!"

He got defensive. "Well, you live with Ian and take showers in the same apartment. The same thing could've happened with you two and I would have believed you if you told me nothing was going on!"

I flushed with embarrassment but also anger. Ignoring his comment, I said, "That's not even the same thing. Alex, you must think I'm an idiot. She confronted me and basically told me you were *with* her. Now you want me to lie to her poor husband because she's a cheating piece of trash? You obviously don't know me very well at all!"

He took a step back, glaring at me. "You're right, Averi. You're absolutely right. I *know* nothing would be going on with you and Ian because he told me he wasn't interested in you and never would be. In fact, he told me the night you texted me to come over when you were so upset. He said he was going to hook up with that girl Ricki and that you meant nothing to him."

My face blazed as tears came to my eyes. "I don't believe he'd ever say that," I whispered.

A strange look came over his face. "Oh my God, you have feelings for him! Is that why you never slept with me? You thought there was a chance with him? Well, let me tell you sweetheart, if he ever made you any promises, don't count on them. His reputation around town is legendary. In fact, he invited me to play pool with him last week and he had women all over him the entire night. I have no doubt he ended up in someone's bed."

I wrenched my arm away from his grip and turned away. "You don't know Ian. He's not like that." I was trying not to cry. "We're very close."

He scoffed. "So, he got what I couldn't get. He *is* the master! All the guys at the station told me not to trust him around you but I told them you were sweet and innocent. Guess I was wrong." His words cut like a knife. "You talk about someone being trash, you should know."

He walked away but at the door he stopped and said, "He'll break your heart, Averi. Karma's a bitch." The door slammed behind him, and I dissolved into tears. I sank into the closest chair and buried my face in my hands.

A little while later, Rochelle came back from lunch, and I faked a stomach bug to leave for the rest of the day. I got in my Jeep and drove to Kendall's. She'd been out of work since her trip to the hospital, and I missed having her right next door.

She answered the door and her face lit up when she saw me. "Averi! What are you doing here? Aren't you supposed to be at work?"

I walked in and sat down on the couch. "I left Rochelle in charge. She's been awesome. I just really needed to talk to you."

She sat down, and I noticed that her huge gauze bandage had been replaced by a butterfly bandage. "What's going on? I know I haven't been there for you lately and I'm really sorry." She placed her hand on mine, and I felt so guilty. Here she was pregnant and injured, and I was here to whine about my love life. I sucked big time.

"Kendall, please don't say you're sorry. You have nothing to be sorry for. I just need my best friend to help sort out my head. How are you feeling by the way?"

She patted my hand then got up to walk into the kitchen. "Well, the morning sickness kicked in but my head feels okay now. So, white or red?" She asked.

Puzzled, I asked, "Huh?"

She laughed. "I'm getting wine." When I began to frown she said, "For *you*. I'm a pregnant non-drinker but I'll grab a glass of water or Kool-Aid depending on your answer in order to join you."

I thought for a moment then said, "White." I heard glasses clinking and a cork pop. "Did you open a new bottle for me?" I shrieked. "Please say you didn't."

She walked back in holding two wine glasses. "It's okay. Tristan will finish it, if you don't. You really need this, I can tell. All right, let's hear it."

I took the wine from her and took a sip. "Mm, Moscato. You rock, sista!"

"Of course," she said with a smile. "Now, spill."

I closed my eyes and sat back in the chair. "Where do I begin?" Opening my eyes to see her reaction, I began with the trip to the lab with Gordon.

"So you've taken the test and now have to wait for the results…that's got to be tough," she said before taking a sip of her water. "Have you talked to your mom?"

I shook my head. "No, we started out playing phone tag so I sent her texts and they kept failing to send. Now, I feel it's better to wait until after we get the results to tell her what I've been doing."

"So, how do you feel about Gordon? If he *is* your dad, you're going to have to decide if you want to let him be a part of your life."

"I know and that's the part that's scaring me. It got real, Kendall. I moved so quickly I didn't think of what comes next," I groaned.

"Averi, I totally understand. That's the part of you I love most though. You're a free spirit…a fly by the seat of your pants girl. You live on instinct and that's what makes you…well, you!"

"Well, I'm starting to question all of my instincts. Lately, they seem to just suck."

She set her glass down on the table. "What's going on with Ian?" She looked at me intently.

"Well, I thought everything was going pretty good." I paused.

"And?" She asked impatiently.

"And...Alex came by today and said some things that are making me doubt everything I believed."

She punched my arm. "Averi Rain! How can you believe anything he says? Misery loves company. He wants you to feel as badly as he does!"

"He told me that Ian said he had no feelings for me, at all." It made me nauseous just to say it. "He said that Ian just wanted to sleep with me and now that he's done it, he'll throw me away."

"Excuse me? How did he know you were together?" She asked.

"I don't know…he guessed? He knew? I don't know. He said that Ian would end up breaking my heart. Kendall, I don't know what to do."

She gave me a look that I was all too familiar with. "Seriously? You need to trust your own judgment. You know he cares about you. Alex is trying to mess with your head and you're letting him!"

My phone chimed in my purse, and I fished it out to see it was a text from Ian.

How'd it go this morning? I've been thinking about you all day. Call me if you're not too busy.

I held up the phone so Kendall could read it. She beamed at me, looking insufferably smug. "What did I just say?" She said, patting herself on the shoulder.

I groaned and threw myself back in the chair. "Why does this have to be so hard?"

"Listen to me," she said as she came over to sit on the arm of the chair. "You are making this hard. Let what happens happen. If it's not meant to be, just pick yourself up and move on. Life's like that." She made perfect sense but there was still that feeling of doubt. "Call him, Averi.

Don't set him up for failure. You have to give him a chance."

I took her hand and gave it a squeeze. "I'm so lucky to have you in my life. You're going to be an amazing mom. I can't wait to find out what you're having so the spoiling can begin."

"Speaking of spoiling, come see what Tristan's done." She took me by the hand and led me to the spare room where there was a pretty good sized pile of baby things sitting in the middle of the bed. "Isn't he a mess?" she asked as she picked up a tiny football in one hand and a baby doll in the other. "He said he's preparing for either."

I laughed and nodded. "Yep, I'm sure he's excited."

"He is, we both are. When the baby gets here, I want you to be the godmother. It would mean the world to me."

"You know I will!" I said giving her a hug. "Well, I guess I'd better head home. I'll call you later."

She walked me to the door. "Just remember Averi…use your instinct," she said seriously.

I had to laugh. "Yes, Master Yoda."

She punched me in the arm. "And don't you forget it!"

Chapter 14

Ian

I was relieved when Averi finally called me. She'd met with Gordon early that morning, and I expected to hear how it went but the lack of texts or calls had me worried. When she did call, she sounded strange, not herself.

"Hey, I'm home," she said when I answered.

"Oh yeah? How did it go?"

She sounded distracted. "Um, well, it was good and I guess we'll know in about five days. Gordon's going to come back when the results are in and we'll find out together."

"Oh good," I said then waited for her to say something, anything. There was an awkward silence. Finally, I said, "Is everything okay?"

"Sure, why wouldn't it be?" She asked defensively.

More silence. "Well, I guess I'll see you when I get home. Do you want me to pick up dinner?" I asked.

"I'm not really hungry. You can get something for yourself. I've got to go. Tiny's got my nook in his mouth." She hung up abruptly. I tossed my phone down on the desk. What in the hell was going on?

When five o'clock rolled around, I stopped on the way home to pick up a pizza in case she'd changed her mind about dinner. When I walked into the apartment, I almost tripped over Tiny, who was laying by the door chewing on a rawhide. He woofed as I stepped over him, and I set the pizza on the counter. I could hear Averi in the bedroom, so I wandered in and saw her in the closet throwing things in piles. "Going somewhere?" I asked laughing.

She stopped and turned to face me. "No, I'm just getting organized. I needed to declutter." She then turned back to the closet and began tossing shoes into a black trash bag.

I watched her body language could see she was tense and obviously upset. "Baby," I said taking her arm to pull her back against me. I wrapped my arms around her and rested my chin on her shoulder. "Talk to me," I whispered. I could feel her trembling and it worried me. "Averi, what's wrong?"

A tear splashed on my arm so I spun her around to make her face me. She had tears rolling down her cheeks. "Ian, I can't do this right now," she choked out.

I was confused. "Do what?"

She shook her head as if arguing with someone in her head. "I can't, I just can't. It's too hard."

I held her at arm's length. "Averi, what are you talking about?"

She finally met my gaze, and it was obvious something was tearing her apart. "Ian, I--" Her voice broke. "I don't want to get hurt."

I slid my hand under her hair to cradle her neck. "Who's going to hurt you? Is this about Gordon? Baby, if this is going to wreck you like this, it's not worth it."

She shook her head. "Not Gordon," she said softly as she looked away.

Something in her tortured expression finally registered. "Me? Is that what you think? That I'll hurt you?" I was incredulous. I saw an almost imperceptible nod. "Averi! What makes you think I'd ever hurt you?" She just stood there sniffling as the tears continued to flow. I pulled her back into my arms wrapping her tightly. "I don't know what brought this on but I promise you, I would *never* hurt you."

She finally quieted and when I released my hold, she grabbed a tissue to wipe her face and blow her nose. "I'm sorry I flipped out." She gave me a sad smile. "I've just got so much going on right now and it's just overwhelming me."

It was breaking my heart to see her like this. Something had changed since last night and I was going to find out what.

I decided to get some air and Tiny was waiting for me to take him out, so I hooked up his leash and took him for a run on the boardwalk. When we got home, I made sure he was taken care of then I tiptoed into the bedroom. Averi was sleeping soundly so I crawled into bed trying not to disturb her. I felt her shift. She turned over, and her arm flopped across my chest. I tucked my arm around her and within a few minutes, I'd fallen asleep as well.

The next morning, I woke to find Averi snuggled against my neck. She still had her arm across my chest and now had her leg wrapped around mine. I moved a little and her eyes cracked open as she started waking up. Covering her mouth as she yawned, she arched her back in a big stretch. "Good morning," she murmured. "Time to get up for work." She climbed out of bed, grabbed some clothes and headed to the shower. My first instinct was to join her in the shower, but I hesitated. Deciding it wasn't the smartest move, I pretended I'd fallen back to sleep and when she came out of the bathroom, and she shook my shoulder. "You need to get up."

I yawned and stretched looking at the clock. "Thanks," I mumbled.

She went into the living room, and I saw through the crack in the door that she had her phone in her hand. I could only assume she was listening to her voicemail then I saw her glance my way. I shaved quickly then jumped in the shower. As I wrapped a towel around my waist, I heard a knock on the door. "Ian?"

As I opened the door, she wrapped her arms around me and lay her head against my chest. "What's wrong, Little Bit?" I said holding her close.

"My whole day sucked and I took it out on you." She gazed up at me with sadness in her eyes. "Thanks for being here."

I sighed giving her a squeeze. "There's nowhere else I'd rather be."

She nodded then pulled away. "Well, I need to get to work and so do you. I'll talk to you later." She walked out and quietly shut the door.

Something definitely changed between us, and not for the better. From that morning on, things were awkward to say the least. It was the longest week of my life. I felt as if she were slipping away, and it was killing me inside.

Each morning, she'd leave early claiming she had clients coming in and every evening as soon as she ate dinner with me, she'd claim she had a headache and go to bed. I still slept beside her and in her sleep, she'd cuddle with me, but as soon as she woke up it was back to the awkward tension again. I tried to talk to Tristan about it, but he didn't know any more than I did. Apparently, Kendall hadn't said anything to him about it either.

Finally, I left work one day and drove to their house. Kendall was sitting on the deck when I arrived. She didn't seem surprised to see me, which made me nervous.

"Hey, how's that baby coming along?" I asked bending down to kiss her cheek.

She smiled. "We're doing fine. Thanks for asking. What are you up to tonight?"

I sat in the chair beside her and stretched my legs out in front of me. "I need to know what's up with Averi." The silence was deafening. "I really need to know, Kendall."

Her smile faded. "She's just got a lot on her right now. You need to be patient."

"Patient? Kendall, I think you know how I feel about her. For the past few days, I've felt like I was living with a stranger."

"Ian, how *do* you feel? Tell me."

"I love her...I really love her." It felt good to say it, and I realized it was the one thing I'd never really said to the one person who needed to hear it. "I've never told her that...I am such an ass."

Kendall laughed softly. "You're not an ass. You've just never had someone you really wanted to say it to. I think that makes it even more special. She's the one, isn't she?"

I nodded. "Yes, she is. She's everything I've ever wanted *and* needed."

She studied me for a moment then said, "I think I know what's on her mind." She began to tell me about Alex's visit with Averi and what he'd told her. The more she said, the angrier I got.

"I'm gonna kill him," I growled.

"Now, Ian. Don't do something you'll regret. I told you this so you can understand where her head is. She's doubting everything right now and you're the only person who can prove what he said wrong."

I stood and started pacing the deck to try to calm down. "Okay, I won't kill him," I said evenly. "I will pay him a visit though. Listen, you take care and I'll call you later." I placed my hand on her shoulder. "I promise I won't do anything drastic."

As I went down the steps, I heard her call out, "Good luck!"

I called my friend at the fire station as I was coming down the stairs and found out that Alex's shift was just about to end. Perfect. I drove over to the station and parked across the street where I could see his truck parked in the lot. Right at seven, he practically came running out to his truck. He had his phone held to his head and was checking his watch. I could only assume he had plans, and unfortunately for him, I was going to have to interrupt them.

I followed him to his apartment and waited until he was inside before I made my way up the stairs to the front door. I listened for a minute and heard him clattering around so I knocked.

"Hang on, baby. Be there in a second!" He called out.

I stood just out of the way of the peephole. I wanted him to be surprised. A couple of minutes later, the door opened, and he popped his head out. He looked to the left first then to the right, and his eyes grew wide when he saw me standing there. He tried to back in and shut the door, but I stuck my foot in before he could. "Hey man!" I said pushing the door open. "I just wanted to talk to you for a minute."

He backed up, eyeing me suspiciously. "What do you want to talk to me about?"

I strolled in casually and clicked the door shut behind me. "Actually, I want two things. First, I want you to tell me exactly what you said to Averi."

He looked around nervously. "I don't know what you're talking about."

I stepped closer. "Yes, I think you do. I know for a fact that you saw Averi last week and said some pretty damning things about me but I want to know exactly what."

He puffed up, his attitude becoming cocky. "It sounds like you already know. And what I told her is the truth! You're nothing but a player and always will be. You'll end up using her and throwing her away just like you've done all the other women you've ever been with. Admit it, Ian, she's just another hookup." I started to speak and then he cut me off. "I do have to say, I'm impressed you got her to give it up. I tried and she just kept putting me off. I really believe it's because she was holding out for you."

I couldn't believe he just went there. "You don't deserve someone like her. And I never tried to sleep with her. I respect her too much to do that."

He scoffed. "But you still got her to do it. Like I said, I'm impressed."

"I'm not going to discuss what has or hasn't happened with Averi. It is none of your business. Now, I'm going to tell you the second thing I came for."

He looked at me curiously. "What would that be?"

I stepped closer. "She deserves an apology."

He nervously took a step back. "And what if I don't want to give her one?"

"Hm, well, then I'll just beat it out of you."

Chapter 15

Averi

The week was unbearable. My head had been so messed up and the one person I needed to talk to was the one person I had doubts about. Ian and I became so close that I'd actually started to believe there was a real future for us but when Alex told me what Ian's real intentions were, I began to question everything he'd said or done. Was it all an elaborate plan to get what he wanted only to dump me later? My mind kept saying, 'He needs a place to live' but my heart kept saying, 'He could have found some other girl to crash with'. I really couldn't think straight and with the paternity results coming any day, I needed to focus on that and deal with Ian later.

Suddenly, out of the blue, I was at the gym when I got a voicemail message from Alex. It was strange and definitely unexpected.

Averi? Hey, it's Alex. I'm probably the last person you want to hear from but I needed to call and apologize. I did you wrong. You are a beautiful and special woman and I never gave you the respect I should have. I'm embarrassed to admit that I cheated on you. You didn't deserve it but that didn't stop me. Another thing I regret is trying to ruin what you have going with Ian. He did tell me he wasn't interested in you but now I know he was only trying to stay out of our relationship. He never flirted with anyone when we went out together...it was all me. That's where I met Diane.

He paused then said, *I'm sorry...for everything.*

The voicemail ended, and I sat staring at the phone for several minutes. I was stunned, mainly because I'd foolishly let someone influence my feelings about Ian. Shame came over me as I thought about how I'd been acting for the last week. He'd been there for me, holding me every night, and I'd turned my back on him. I needed to talk to him. I was getting ready to call when I got a text.

Hey, I've got to go to Charlotte for a couple of days to cover a project for Tristan. They booked my flight for me and it leaves in two hours. I'm sorry I missed you when I came home to pack. I'll try to call you when I land.

My eyes blurred with tears as I texted back.

Okay, we need to talk when you get home. Be safe.

He responded right away.

Sounds serious. Everything okay?

This definitely was not a text conversation.

Yes, it can wait.

He sent me back a smiley.

I called Kendall but Tristan answered her phone. "Hey Averi," he said softly.

"Hey, is Kendall around? I really need to talk to her."

Still keeping his voice low he said, "She's sleeping. She's been having a tough time with morning sickness…in fact it's all day. Can I have her call you when she wakes up?"

"Sure, it's no emergency. Just tell her to take care of herself."

"Will do. And if you need anything, let me know. Ian told me to check on you while he's out of town."

I smiled. "Thanks, I will." I shuffled into the bedroom and threw myself on the bed, my phone clutched in my hand and within minutes, I was fast asleep.

Tiny woke me with a wet kiss to the nose, and I quickly checked my phone to find that Ian had called me, and I'd slept right through it! "Damn it!" I said throwing my phone down onto the bed. Tiny grabbed it in his mouth and took off into the living room. "Tiny! Come back here!" I jumped up and chased after him. It became a standoff for me and a game for him. He tried to squeeze under the futon, but he'd become so big he couldn't fit. I reached to take the phone, but he turned his head taking it just out of my reach. "Tiny, please give Mommy her phone," I pleaded. Suddenly, it started ringing and he flung it in surprise where it ended up in the corner. I scrambled to get it.

Checking it quickly to see who it was, I saw a number I didn't recognize. "Hello?" I asked breathlessly.

"Is this…Averi Rain?" A female voice asked.

"Yes, it is."

"Great! This is Laura Holman and I'm calling to let you know that we have the results from your test and want to schedule an appointment to give those to you."

Just hearing those words made me start trembling. "Um, great. I'll have to call you right back."

"Ok, that's fine." She hung up and I immediately called Gordon.

"Hey, kiddo!" He said brightly.

"Hi…" I paused. "We have our results."

"Can you hold on?" There was silence on the other end for a few minutes. "I'll be there this afternoon. I just booked my flight and it leaves in three hours. I should be in Wilmington by two. I'll call you when I land."

I couldn't speak. I realized my heart was beating rapidly, and I was on the verge of an anxiety attack.

"Averi? Are you okay?" He asked with concern.

I tried to calm myself. "Yeah," I managed.

"I know this is scary, it is for me too," he said softly. "I'll see you in a bit. It's going to be fine."

I nodded silently then disconnected the call. I called Laura back and set up our appointment then as I hung up my phone, I thought about Ian. I scrolled through my recent calls and found Ian's number. My finger was poised to call him, but I couldn't do it. I wanted to kick my own ass for being so stupid. Ian was nothing but good to me, and I let Alex get in my head and screw it all around.

Instead of calling him, I called Rochelle. When I explained what was happening, she was more than happy to cover for me. To relax, I took a leisurely bubble bath to try to relax and took extra time on my hair. Digging through my closet, I pulled out a white cotton shirt then grabbed a pair of hot pink capris. I checked the time and saw it was almost two. I took Tiny outside to keep my mind off of things for a few minutes and was coming back upstairs when my phone rang.

"Hey, I'm in a cab headed to the lab now," Gordon said when I answered.

I took a deep breath and said, "I'm on my way."

When I drove up in front of the lab, Gordon was already there standing outside. He gave me a huge smile when he saw me and once again helped me out of my Jeep. "You look pale," he said with concern. "Are you feeling okay?"

I had to be honest. "I feel queasy but I know it's from nerves. I'll be okay. Let's do this."

We waited only a few minutes before we were led to a private room. Instead of a traditional doctor's office, this room was more homey and warm. It had a leather couch and two oversized easy chairs, and the wall was lined with bookcases. I picked up a magazine and started flipping through it while he paced the room looking at the books filling the shelves. We both jumped when the door opened, and a gray haired man walked in.

"Good afternoon," he said holding his hand out to Gordon. "Mr. Haynes, I'm Dr. Sampson." They shook hands then he turned to me. "And you must be Ms. Rain." He shook my hand as well and then he gestured for us to sit. "So, we're here to find out if you are father and daughter." We both nodded and he continued. "Well, let's see," he said shuffling though several pages in a manila folder. He seemed to find what he was looking for then looked up at us. "Mr. Haynes, in the paternity of Averi Rain, you *are* her father to a 99.99% probability."

We both sat in stunned silence for several minutes and the doctor patiently waited for the news to sink in. Finally, Gordon said in a choked voice, "Thank you." Tears flowed down his cheeks.

I swallowed hard to keep from sobbing but when I saw him crying, I lost it. He gripped my hand tightly and then wrapped his arm around my shoulder. I leaned against him and sobbed into his shirt. The doctor walked over and placed his hand on my shoulder and tucked a tissue into my hand. "Every time I give people this news, I walk away knowing that lives have changed. Whether that's a good thing or a bad thing is up to you. I'll leave you two alone."

I heard the door close behind him, and we just sat there together. A few minutes before we were acquaintances, and now we were family. My dad, this man was my dad! My own flesh and blood. The tears finally stopped, and I wiped my face with the tissue and blew my nose.

"So," I sniffled. "What do we do now?"

He smiled. "Let's start with dinner and we'll go from there."

We made our way to Wrightsville Beach to the Bluewater Grill. The hostess seated us on the waterfront patio, and we sat there quietly watching the boats coming in to the dock. The server brought us some wine, and as I took a sip, I said, "I'm so overwhelmed. Do you feel that way?"

He nodded. "I really am. Not only did I learn I have a beautiful daughter," he said clinking his glass to mine, "I just realized how much I've missed out on…and it breaks my heart."

Shaking my head, I said, "I really don't know why she did this."

He placed his hand on mine. "I'm sure she had her reasons. It just kills me that all these years have been wasted."

The server came with our food so our conversation was interrupted but as soon as she left us alone, I said, "I want to call her and tell her what we've done but I'm scared."

He nodded. "I understand that completely but I also think you need to tell her as soon as possible."

I sighed. "I guess the sooner the better." I got up from the table. "I need a little privacy." I walked over down the pier and sat down on the edge to call my mom.

"Averi! It's about time you called me! I was worried to death but then again, I knew if anything serious was going on, Kendall would've called me. It's been so busy since we got here and we don't have the best cell service at the house. We're still trying to get another car but that takes time so I've been stuck at the house in the middle of nowhere. I was waiting to hear back from you but figured you were just really busy."

When she finally took a breath, I stopped her. "Mom, I need to talk to you…it's something really important."

She was silent for a moment then said, "You're not pregnant are you? I know we've always been open about things and try not to be nosy about who you're intimate with, but I thought we made it clear that if you were, you'd be responsible."

"Mom, no! I'm not pregnant. I--"

"Oh thank God! I know you've been seeing that young man, Alex, and that was the first thing that popped in my head." She paused. "I'd hope you would have better sense than to let yourself get pregnant with someone you weren't serious with…"

I jumped in, "Like you did?"

There was a long period of silence. Finally, I heard her stammer, "Wha—what do you mean? Your father and I were married when you were born."

I wanted to cry, but I held it together. "Yes, I know you and dad were married when I was born…but there was someone else, wasn't there? Before Dad?"

"Averi, what are you saying? Has someone been trying to fill your head with lies because I don't appreciate the implication? Where are you going with this?" Her voice became shrill.

I took a deep breath then said, "Does the name Gordon Haynes mean anything to you?" The silence was deafening. I thought for a moment that she'd hung up, but as I listened closely, I could hear her ragged breathing. "Mom? Does it?" I asked softly.

"Honey, I don't know what lies he's told you but…"

"Mom, we did a paternity test and we got the results today."

"And you didn't think you needed to tell me this?" she asked in a disheartened voice. "You went behind my back…where was our trust?"

"Mom, I didn't tell you because there was nothing to tell. I didn't know if he was my dad and I did what an adult would do…we did the test and got the results. He *is* my dad. Now, I want to know why you lied to him all those years ago and why you've lied to me."

Her voice rose, "Averi, I'm still your mother and I don't like your tone."

My voice rose to match hers. "My tone? Mom, everything I've believed has been a lie. Daddy will always be my dad but I have a biological father who wants to be a part of my life."

She scoffed. "Is that what he told you? Averi, mark my words, he'll do you wrong just like he did me."

Finally, she was admitting it without realizing it. "What did he do, Mom? You say he did you wrong but what did he do? We've talked about this and he has no idea."

"Well, he's not going to admit anything. He broke my heart all those years ago and I just paid him back." She sounded so angry.

I became irate. "You paid him back by keeping me from him? By lying to him and saying I wasn't his? That's just cruel, Mom."

"Averi, you don't know what happened. You have no right to judge what I did!" She cried.

I kept my voice even. "Whatever your reasons, it was wrong. Look, I've got to go. Gordon's waiting for me."

She shrieked, "He's there? He's with you now?"

I sighed. "Yes, Mom. He came to get the results with me. When you calm down and decide to tell me the whole story, call me. I'll be willing to listen but not now. Goodbye."

I hung up and closed my eyes. I could feel the tears threatening, but my anger kept them in check. Gordon came up behind me placing his hand on my shoulder.

"Still angry, huh?" asked shaking his head. "I wish I knew what I did."

"Honestly, I don't know. She's convinced herself that she did the right thing but won't tell me what happened. Who knows, maybe someday she'll realize I'm an adult and I deserve to know the truth." I placed my hand on his. "In the meantime, I'll give her time to absorb this and the next move is hers."

He nodded. "I think we'll both have to be patient. I've got to explain to my wife and daughter as well and really don't know what I'm going to say." He leaned against the railing. "I think the part that will make it easier for them to accept is the fact that I had no idea you were my daughter." He smiled broadly. "My daughter, Averi…has a nice ring to it."

I returned the smile. "I think so, too."

It was getting late and he needed to check into his hotel, so I dropped him off and then headed home. When I got to the apartment, I called Kendall and told her everything.

Naturally, she was excited for me but also sad because she knew this would change a lot of things in my life. As I recounted my mom's words and reaction, her anger was the one thing that perplexed me. I was bound and determined to find out what happened between them right before I was born.

As I hung up the phone, I checked to see if I had any missed calls or texts from Ian but there were none. I began to wonder if my behavior the past week had pushed him away. I lay with Tiny curled up next to me and let all the emotions I'd been holding back come out in a flood of tears until I fell into an exhausted sleep.

The sound of knocking on my door startled me, and I jumped out of bed, stubbing my toe on the dresser. I glanced at the clock and saw it was a little after nine but it felt much later. I peered out the peephole and was shocked to find my mom standing at the door.

"Mom! What are you doing here?" I blurted.

She walked to me and wrapped me in a tight hug. Her voice breaking, she said, "I drove here to tell you that I'm sorry and to tell you the whole story. Ever since you told me you found out about your dad, I've been kicking myself for lying to you all these years."

Eyes downcast, my mom slumped down in the chair, and I sat cross-legged on the floor in front of her. "Before we do this…I need to ask you something." She looked up and placing my hand on her knee, I asked, "Can I call Gordon so we could talk everything over together?"

Her face flushed bright red. "Averi, I'm so embarrassed. I don't know if I can face him."

"Mom," I said softly, "he's a really great person and I believe he just wants answers like I do."

Closing her eyes she sighed, "Okay, you can call him."

I grabbed my phone and Gordon picked up on the first ring. "Hey, sweetie," he said cheerfully. "What's up?"

I hesitated for a moment then said, "Mom's here."

Silence greeted me from the other end of the line. "Lottie," he breathed.

"Yeah, she's here and I think you should come over. She's ready to tell the whole story and I think we need to hear it together."

He sighed. "I'll be there in ten minutes."

I made us some tea and my mom nervously sipped at it, her eyes glancing at the clock, no doubt counting down the minutes. When a knock came at the door, she jumped almost spilling her cup.

I hopped up to get the door and could see Gordon was as nervous as Mom was. I gave him a hug and a reassuring smile then led him into the living room. My mom was visibly trembling and pale, obviously distressed but instead of an angry confrontation, Gordon took her hand and brought it to his lips. "It's good to see you, Lottie," he murmured against her fingers. Releasing her hand, he walked over to sit on the futon.

Looking at my mom who was on the verge of tears, I said, "It's time."

Her bottom lip trembling, she began to tell us what happened. "I shouldn't have lied to you Gordon," she said tears brimming in her eyes. "I was just so hurt that I felt that I needed to make you suffer."

"You were hurt? Lottie, what did I do to hurt you?" He asked with a puzzled expression on his face.

Swallowing hard, she blurted, "You cheated on me! I saw you Gordon…you and that piece of trash, Jill, in the bedroom at Greg's house after the championship football game."

His eyebrows knitted together as he frowned. "Lottie, I don't know what you're talking about. I was at the party waiting for you. I don't know what you saw but Jill and I were *not* together. As a matter of fact, she was dating Billy Thompson and, if I remember correctly, we went in the bedroom for some privacy because she wanted to find out if he had any plans to pop the question." My mom's mouth moved wordlessly as he continued. "Lottie, I have to ask, did you know you were pregnant when you broke up with me?"

Eyes downcast, she nodded. "I was going to tell you that night but then I saw you two and I was so upset, I just couldn't. When I ran from the party, I bumped into Sheryl Martin. She asked me why I was crying and when I explained, she told me that you and Jill had been seeing each other for months."

Gordon shook his head and sighed. "Sheryl Martin. Well there's someone with an axe to grind. Lottie, she was one of the managers for the football team and had made it very clear she was interested in me. One day after practice, after everyone had left, she came on to me in the gym. I emphatically told her I was in love with you and only you. I could tell she was mad and she'd stomped away saying something about getting me back but I had no idea she would do something so diabolical."

Tears began to stream down my mom's cheeks, and I quickly handed her a tissue. "Gordon, I should've talked to you. I know that now. I got a job to try to support myself and the baby I was going to have. That's when I met Dennis. He was the manager at the restaurant where I was working. We became friends. He knew I was pregnant but never asked any questions. He made it clear that he would be willing to take care of me and my baby as if it were his own. My heart still belonged to you but I also knew this was an opportunity I couldn't pass up. I knew he was a good person and that I'd grow to love him, which I have. When Averi was born, I put Dennis on the birth certificate knowing it wasn't true." She turned to me and held out her hand which I took. "She looked so much like you when she was born that it broke my heart. To everyone else, she looked like me and eventually people began to say she looked like Dennis so I felt confident my secret was safe."

Gordon looked at me and smiled. "You know, I really believe it was fate that I walked into her shop that day."

Wiping her eyes, my mom shook her head in disbelief. "How did you even put it together?" She asked.

I jumped in with the explanation. "We have the same eyes."

She smiled and nodded. "They're gorgeous and really are unique."

"The minute I saw her eyes and then she told me who her mother was, I just knew. The hardest part for me was deciding whether or not to pursue it and risk messing up her life. Finally, I just wrote the letter and left it in her hands." He put his hand on my shoulder giving it a squeeze. "I'm just so thankful she wanted to find out."

I put my hand on his and gave it a pat. "Nothing has changed, Mom. I still love Daddy and he'll always be that to me. He's been there for me all my life and always will be but now I have a family history." I turned to Gordon and grinned. "I also have a sister that I hope I'll get to know someday."

He nodded. "I hope so, too. I want to tell them in person so as soon as I get home, I'll let them know what's going on."

My mom's eyes grew sad. "All those years, I hated you and had no reason to. I can't say I'm sorry enough. I hope you'll forgive me…both of you."

Gordon stood and pulled my mom into a hug. "Who knows how our lives would have turned out but what's past is past. We have a beautiful daughter and that's all that matters."

After we visited a little while longer, he left to go back to his hotel, and I insisted mom spend the night. We spent the evening talking until we were both too tired to talk anymore.

The next morning, before she left to go back to Boone, I sat down and wrote my dad a letter and made her promise to give it to him as soon as she saw him. After I walked her to her car, I strolled along the boardwalk enjoying the solitude before the crowds would come claiming their spot on the beach for the day, then it was back to work. I tried not to think about the fact that Ian hadn't called me, but it wouldn't get out of my head. I went into work hoping that would distract me but as the day dragged on, I knew it was useless.

Chapter 16

Ian

"They've been stolen!" I announced to the police officer standing at the door of my hotel room.

"Calm down, sir. I need to know exactly what was stolen." He pulled out an iPad and began to type.

Explaining to him that after checking in my room, I'd decided to run down to the hotel restaurant to grab a bite to eat. Both my computer and phone batteries needed charging so I'd plugged them in before going downstairs. When I'd come back to my room only an hour later, I noticed that my bag was dumped out on the bed, and my computer and phone were both missing. I distinctly remembered pulling the door closed so my assumption was the thief had to be someone with a key.

The police officer took all of my information and then advised me to call my phone company to have my phone shut off to prevent anyone from using it, which I did. I was thankful that my laptop didn't have anything crucial on it, but it was fairly new and hadn't been cheap. The manager of the hotel came to the room and apologized for my trouble and offered to comp my bill for my entire stay and said the hotel security was going through the surveillance tapes to see if they could pinpoint what happened. The worst part of losing my phone was that I didn't have anyone's numbers and like most cell phone users, didn't have them memorized. Also I had no computer to email anyone and would just have to wait until I got to the office for my meeting.

A car came to pick me up to take me to the bank located in downtown Charlotte. I'd never been to the area before and was struck by its beauty. We passed the Bank of America Stadium where the Panthers play and I spotted the Nascar Hall of Fame in the skyline. We pulled up in front of a skyscraper bearing the name of our sister bank. As I climbed from the car, I was greeted by a young man named Russell who, from what Tristan had told me, was his replacement when he'd left to come back home.

"Ian?" he asked extending his hand. "Welcome. Mr. Davenport is expecting you," he said with a smile. He led me to the elevator where we rode to the top floor. The elevator opened into a large conference room, and I saw a group of people already gathered. They stopped talking when we walked in, and I felt a bit nervous but then I saw a familiar face.

"Ian! It's good to see you again." Jay Anderson held out his hand giving me a firm handshake. "How are Tristan and Kendall?"

"Great, they're doing just great. Tristan would've been here but Kendall had a fall and he's been staying close to home until she recovers."

He nodded. "That's exactly where he needs to be." Smiling, he turned to pull a beautiful brunette forward to meet me. "Ian, this is Callie Brisson. She's my partner in our firm."

Callie looked me up and down and said, "So you're Tristan's little brother, huh? Good looks do run in the family!" She took me by the arm and led me to a chair. I felt completely awkward and obviously she could tell. Laughing, she said, "I'm just messing with you. I was so disappointed we didn't get to go to their wedding. Tristan told me to harass you when I finally got to meet you."

Sighing with relief, I grinned. "Sounds like something he'd do."

An older gentleman I assumed was Mr. Davenport came in the room followed by Russell. He walked around the table shaking everyone's hand to welcome them. When it was my turn, he studied me for a moment then said, "You have got to be Ian. You must get your good looks from your older brother."

Seriously, I said, "That's funny, everyone usually says he gets them from me."

He appeared puzzled for a moment then he broke into a huge smile. "You got me! That was a good one." Everyone else in the room started laughing, and I mentally patted myself on the back for being charming with the big boss.

The purpose of the meeting was to coordinate a renovation project to make the interior of the building in Wilmington match the new design of the building in Charlotte. Since Jay and Callie's firm had done the original designs, they were going to head the project redoing my bank. My job was to be a liaison between the firm in Charlotte and the contractors in Wilmington and handle any financial transfers for the building costs. It was a really exciting opportunity for me. I became so wrapped up in the planning that the day flew by before I knew it.

"So, Ian. Do you have plans for the evening? Going out on the town as you single guys do?" Jay asked as we rode the elevator down to the lobby at the end of the day.

I shook my head and chuckled. "No, I was going to head back to my hotel and catch a movie."

"Well," he said stopping in the lobby. "You're welcome to come to eat dinner with us as long as you don't mind a little girl talking your ears off. And before you say it's too much trouble for Jane, she's the one who mentioned it."

I protested. "But isn't she due any day?" Thinking back to Tristan and Kendall's wedding and how pregnant Jane had been, I figured she had to be on the verge of delivery.

He smiled. "No, we've got about two more weeks before Olivia arrives. Really, it's not an imposition at all."

I shrugged and laughed. "Sounds like a sweet deal! Let's go!"

Jay drove me over to their house which was on the outskirts of Charlotte. It was a really beautiful home set in an older neighborhood. When we pulled into the driveway, Jay honked the horn and a moment later, Jane and little Jolene came out to greet us.

"Daddy! You're home!" Jolene squealed. She rushed to him throwing herself into his arms. He swung her around and gave her a big kiss on the cheek. She giggled as she wrapped her arms around his neck to give him a big squeeze. After a moment, she noticed me. "Hi…" she said shyly. Jane walked up to wrap her hand around Jay's arm, watching with amusement.

"Jolene, do you remember Ian? He's Tristan's brother…you met him at their wedding," Jane said as Jay set her down.

She looked up at me and giggled. "I love Tristan. Did he come with you?"

I knelt down to her level. "No, I'm sorry, he didn't. He's at home with Kendall taking care of her."

Her eyes grew wide. "Is she okay? I like her. She has pretty hair." She took me by the hand and started to pull me toward the house.

Following behind, Jane asked, "Ian? Is everything okay?"

Nodding, I said, "Yeah, she fell and hit her head. She ended up with some stitches and…found out she's pregnant."

Jane's mouth fell open. "Wow that was some bump on the head!" We all started laughing except for Jolene who stared at us with a frown.

"I don't get it, Mommy," she said pouting.

Jane put her hand on the top of Jolene's head. "Sweetie, it was a grown up joke. You know what we've said about those."

Jolene nodded seriously. "Yes, you said I'll know what it means when I'm twenty-one. That's a long time to wait to find out what you're talking about. I'll probably forget by then." That really made us laugh which made her even more frustrated. "No fair, no fair. Grownups have all the fun!"

Jay smiled as he watched her run up the stairs to her room. "If she only knew how wrong that statement was."

After a wonderful evening complete with dinner, a round of Hungry Hippos and a Barbie dress up party, Jay drove me back to the hotel. They'd been so nice to me, and I appreciated a home cooked meal versus the local Micky D's. I was about to get out of the car when I remembered I had no phone or laptop. "Hey Jay, do you happen to have

Tristan's number?" I asked. He did and jotted it down on an old receipt.

When I got to my room, I used the hotel phone to call Tristan, who then gave me Averi's number. I called her but got no answer and when it went to voicemail, it said her mailbox was full and wouldn't let me leave a message. Dejected and tired, I threw myself on my bed and fell asleep.

My alarm woke me the next morning and groggily, I realized I was still in my work clothes. Crawling from the bed to the shower, I hastily shaved and showered just making it downstairs for the car service to take me to the office. Another busy day followed along with another dinner invitation, this time from Callie and Justin. We had a really nice dinner at a local Italian restaurant and when I got back to my room, I got a message at the desk that they'd found my laptop in one of the janitorial closets, but my phone was nowhere to be found. Once I had my computer back, I checked it over and found it to be unharmed. I spent the rest of the evening packing for my trip home in the morning. Having my laptop back, I had the internet at my fingertips again, and so I began my search. Within seconds, I'd found exactly what I was looking for. Averi wasn't going to know what hit her.

Jay picked me up the next morning to take me to the airport. We pulled through a drive-thru to grab some coffee and suddenly Jay said, "So...Callie and I were very impressed with how you handled the meetings the past couple of days. If you're interested, there's a job as our financial coordinator available."

Surprised, I turned to him and said, "Wow! I didn't see that coming at all! In all honesty, I'd love to work with you both but there's someone special back home and I can't leave her. I appreciate the offer, I really do. You guys are awesome."

He nodded and smiled. "I understand. When you find someone special, you really need to grab 'em and hold on tight. I knew Jane was special right away and wanted to be with her and Jolene as a family. There's nothing more amazing than having that kind of love and connection."

"Yeah," I said taking a sip of my coffee. "I guess I've always loved Averi, I just had to grow up and become the man she deserves. I only hope she feels the same way."

We drove to the Charlotte airport and as he dropped me off, he said, "We look forward to working with you on this project. We'll be in touch."

"Thanks," I said as I shook his hand, then grabbed my bag and headed into the terminal.

After an hour-long flight, we landed in Wilmington, and I grabbed a cab to take me right to the cell phone store to get a new phone and thankfully, all of my contacts were hanging out in my cloud so within a few minutes, I had a new phone and was in another cab and on my way. The first person I called was Kendall and thankfully, she was feeling better and was back at work. She told me that Averi was definitely working, and that she'd been pretty busy. I'd just hung up when my phone rang with an unfamiliar number.

"Hello?" I answered.

"Mr. O'Neal? This is Sergeant Bacon from the Charlotte PD. I'm calling to inform you that we apprehended the person who stole your property. It turned out to be a maintenance person who'd been fired for misconduct and apparently, he'd made himself a passkey before he left. He'd been lucky until the surveillance camera caught him this time. We recovered your phone and will send it to you at the address we have on file."

"Okay, sounds good. I'm just glad you caught him. If you need me for anything, please let me know."

"Will do and thank you sir," he replied.

My cab dropped me off around the corner from the building, and I ran up to the apartment. Tiny, who wasn't so tiny anymore was whining to be let out when I walked in. He began to sniff me and rub himself against my legs. "You still love me, little man?" I asked as I tossed my suitcases in the closet and threw on some jeans and a t-shirt. He followed me from room to room with my old shoe in his mouth. "Give me that!" I said laughing. "We're going for a walk."

On our way to the boardwalk, I realized I had forgotten to get her some flowers, so I improvised by picking some wildflowers from an empty lot on the way. Tiny dragged me down to the pier where I found a bench to sit on to wait. I didn't have to wait long for the drone of an engine, and as I shielded my eyes, I could make out the shape of an airplane making its way down the beach. It was towing a banner, and as it went by, several people on the pier who knew me were pointing at me and smiling so I gave them a thumbs up. I watched the plane travel all the way down the beach and circle back around to make its way over town. My phone started ringing.

"Hey man! I just saw a banner with your name on it fly by my guard stand," my friend Wyatt said laughing.

"Pretty cool, huh?" I asked laughing.

"Yeah, if I didn't know any better, I'd think you're off the market and letting it be known in no uncertain terms!"

"Well, that's exactly what I'm doing…and I hope it works!

He laughed again. "Good luck, man!"

A few minutes passed then my friend who was flying the plane texted me that he was on his way back around. With a deep breath and a prayer, I called Kendall.

Chapter 17

Averi

Two days and not a word. I felt as if someone had kicked me in the gut. How could I have been so stupid? Ian probably thought I was a complete moron, and I had no one but myself to blame.

I had just finished a piercing and was ringing up the sale when my phone rang.

"Averi!" Kendall yelled. "You've got to go outside! You're not going to believe it!"

"What? Believe what?" I asked. "Is something wrong?" Holding my phone to my ear, I walked to the front window and peered out.

"Are you outside yet?" She persisted. "You need to go outside!" She obviously wanted me outside.

"Dude, calm yourself!" I laughed. "I can't go all the way out, there's nobody here but me!"

"Averi, you lock that door and get your ass outside right now!" She growled.

I stopped laughing. "Okay, I'm going…no need to get nasty!"

"You haven't seen nasty. Get moving, now!" She hung up and I stood staring at the phone wondering what had come over her.

Curious, I grabbed my keys, flipped over my sign and locked up. I walked out onto the boardwalk and looked both ways but couldn't see anything out of the ordinary. There were kids playing in the surf and people sunbathing on their brightly colored towels. I was just about to call her back and cuss her out for scaring me to death when someone walking by said, "That's probably the sweetest thing I've ever seen."

As I turned, another person walked by and said, "What a lucky young lady." Okay, this was becoming Twilight Zone-ish.

I was just about to ask them what they meant when I got another call from Kendall. "Why are you looking this way? Turn around and look up! Sheesh!" She hung up.

At that moment, I heard the drone of an airplane but couldn't see anything. I shielded my eyes with my hand and could just make out the outline of a plane pulling a banner. Making my way down to the beach, I walked to the edge of the water to get a better view.

As the plane got closer, I started to make out the words on the banner, and my heart began to hammer in my chest.

IAN O'NEAL LOVES AVERI RAIN

I couldn't breathe. I stumbled back and landed on my butt in the sand. Ian loves me? Was this a joke or something?

"It's true, you know."

I heard his voice and I slowly turned to see Ian and Tiny standing behind me. I jumped up, brushing the sand from my backside, my face flushed with emotion. "Did you do that?" I asked breathlessly.

His icy blue eyes were locked on mine as he said, "Yes, I did and I do."

I wanted to hear the words. "You do what?" I asked softly.

"I love you, Averi. More than you'll ever know."

Tears welled up and I bit my lip to hold back a sob. "You love me?" It seemed like a dream.

He slowly stepped toward me, his eyes never leaving mine. "I love everything about you. I love your beauty, your spirit and most importantly…your heart." From behind his back, he pulled out a bouquet of delicate wildflowers. "Tiny and I got these for you." Tiny was circling us excitedly and had his leash wrapped around our legs pulling us closer together. Our bodies were now inches apart.

"They're perfect," I whispered.

"Perfect, like you," he said brushing my hair from my eyes.

All fear and doubt evaporated, and I said the words I'd always wanted to say to him, "I love you, Ian." His face broke into a huge smile. He wrapped his arms around me and kissed me passionately. Tiny was barking at us, and we broke apart laughing. "I think he's happy for us," I said rubbing Tiny behind his ear.

Ian unwrapped the leash from our legs. "Let's go home. I need to show my lady how much I missed her." He gave his eyebrows a wiggle making me laugh. "Then I need to find out what I missed when I was gone…but first things first."

Back in the apartment, as soon as we made sure Tiny was secure, he backed me into the bedroom up against the wall, holding my arms above my head, his lips finding the sweet spot on my neck. "I missed this, baby," he growled, his breath warm on my skin. "You're so soft, it makes me crazy."

I couldn't find my breath, and I arched against him wanting more. He feathered kisses up my jaw to find my mouth where he began to kiss me softly. As I parted my lips, his tongue touched mine, and I gasped and freed my hands to tangle them in his hair. He cupped my face, sweeping his thumb across my cheek sending shivers through my body.

His tongue swept across my lower lip then he gave me another soft, gentle kiss. Our eyes opened simultaneously, and he leaned in to whisper in my ear, "Averi, take me to bed…"

I whispered back, "Only if it's forever." He carried me to the bedroom and with his foot, gently shut the door.

Being with Ian this time was free of doubt and full of love. The emotional and physical connection between us was pure and as we kissed and touched each other, I finally began to understand what a soul mate really was. Every nerve ending in my body was on fire as his hands gently touched my skin. He trailed his lips down my neck murmuring against my skin, "Mm, I love you." He looked up into my eyes and whispered, "Forever."

Later, as we lay tangled in the sheets, our arms wrapped around each other, he pushed my dampened hair from my face and kissed my flushed cheek. "That felt so right," he said softly.

I placed my hand against his cheek feeling the scruff of his beard. I kissed him gently and nodded. He tucked me into his chest his hands softly trailing up and down my bare back. "Baby, for the first time in my life, I feel complete."

My face pressed against his chest, his heart thudding against me, I nodded. "I always hoped you'd love me…I just didn't think it could really happen." When I said that, he pulled me even tighter.

"I was such an idiot. For the longest time, I wanted to tell you and when I finally decided to, you'd met Alex. I'll admit, it made me crazy to see you with him. He wasn't good enough for you." He tilted my face up to look at him. "I need you like the air I breathe. Being away from you even for a couple of days was torture. I couldn't wait to get back and tell you how I felt." His voice broke, and I saw the shimmer of tears in his eyes.

I propped myself up on my elbow and trailed my fingers along his brow. "Honestly, I missed you like crazy too. I really needed you but was too afraid to call."

"What happened? Are you okay?" He asked running his fingers through my hair.

"I got the results from the paternity test," I said softly.

Abruptly, he sat up. "You did? I wasn't here! What happened?"

Taking a deep breath I said, "He's my dad."

His eyes searched mine. "How do you feel about it?" He asked.

"I feel pretty good," I admitted. "My mom came to town and they talked it out. It turns out it was just a huge misunderstanding that changed their lives. I don't ever want that to happen with us." I paused, then continued. "On that note, I have a confession to make. Do you remember the night you asked me to meet you at The Pelican and I never showed up?"

"You mean right before you started hating my guts?" He said smiling, before placing a soft kiss on my forehead.

"Yeah, so the reason I was so upset was I walked in and saw you with someone." I blurted.

He frowned. "Averi, I haven't been with anyone else."

I sighed. "You were standing at the bar with a redhead and she had her arms wrapped around you. I assumed--"

He interrupted me. "You assumed but it wasn't what you thought. I remember who that was now...her name is Lauren and she's Hobie's niece. She was celebrating her bachelorette party that night. I was actually telling her how I'd met someone special and I was hoping to introduce you."

I groaned and tried to pull away. "So, I almost ended up making a huge mistake, like my mom did all those years ago."

Ian pulled me to him and wrapping me in his arms, kissed me softly. "Averi, the difference is, I didn't give up. I love you and no matter what, you've got me. The only thing that matters now is that we're together. You're stuck with me, I'm afraid."

I kissed him tenderly, then whispered, "There's nowhere else I'd rather be."

Epilogue

Averi

Turning back to the mirror, I checked my reflection one last time. I loved my dress because it was so me. A little bit traditional and a lot non-traditional, it was definitely my style. It was an ivory mermaid dress with a white sheer overlay embroidered with off-white flowers of different sizes, the perfect dress for a beach wedding.

Adjusting the flowers in my hair, I turned to look back at Kendall who was getting Patrick dressed for the wedding. He was more intent on pulling her hair than cooperating and as she struggled with the snaps on his onesie she looked up at me laughing. "He's just like his father," she giggled.

I walked over to give him a kiss on the forehead, and he instantly became enthralled with my hair instead, which I quickly got out of his hand before it went in his mouth. "He's a typical man already? Is that what you're saying?"

We laughed and then as a team managed to dress him in his tiny suit for the wedding.

We heard a knock at the door and my mom's voice said, "Girls, you've got about fifteen minutes."

"You can come in," I called out. "We're just dressing the baby."

My mom opened the door and poked her head in. "Oh Averi, you look absolutely beautiful." Tears shone in her eyes, and I saw her try to blink them back. "Look what you've done…now my makeup's going to be all over my face."

I grinned. "What's a wedding day without the mother of the bride in tears? Isn't it good luck or something?" I walked over to give her a tight hug.

"Well, if my tears will bring you luck, you'll be the luckiest couple in history because I can promise you, I'll be like a fountain."

"You'll be fine, Mom," I said picking up my bouquet of wildflowers from the bed. "I got you a box of tissues for the ceremony. They're by your seat."

"You thought of everything, didn't you?" she asked, laughing through her tears. "I thought it was a perfect idea to have your dad and Gordon walk you down the aisle together."

"Well, I wanted them both to have the experience and that was a perfect solution. By the way, where is Brianna? Have you seen her?"

The door to the bedroom opened and she came rushing in. "Sorry, I walked out of the hotel and forgot my flip flops. Thank goodness Dad drove me back to get them." She twirled in front of me to model her purple mini-dress. "I love this dress!" she squealed. "And thanks for talking Dad into letting me color my hair to match it!"

I laughed. "Bri, I didn't talk him into anything. He just accepts the fact that he has two daughters that have the same quirky taste."

"And I have to say," she said giving me a hug, "I have the best sister in the world."

I felt a lump in my throat, and I blew out a breath to keep from crying. "Takes one to know one, kiddo," I said, my voice breaking.

Another knock came at the door interrupting us. "Babe, I can take Patrick now," Tristan said through the door.

Kendall handed him through to her husband and then quickly retouched her makeup and hair. She glanced at the clock and grinned. "It's time!"

We made our way down the boardwalk, and I paused at the top of the steps leading to the beach. My daddy and Gordon, who I now called Dad, were waiting for me on the sand, huge smiles stretched across their faces. I carefully descended the steps, and as I stepped onto the sand, I hooked one arm around my daddy's and one around my dad's. Brianna and Kendall slowly began to walk down the aisle and when the director gave us our cue, we followed them. The guests were standing so my view of Ian was blocked at first but when we got closer, I found him and our eyes locked. Giving me a nod, he smiled brightly. When we finally got to the arbor, I wanted to jump into his arms but unfortunately, I had to be patient.

The past year had been so amazing. After we'd made it clear we were both committed to each other, our lives only got better. I realized that in order to have a future with Ian, I needed to learn to trust him and not jump to crazy conclusions every time a woman talked to him.

He thrived in his new job and one of the first things he did was to pay Tristan back all the money he'd paid for rent from their wager. We found a roomier apartment not too far from the boardwalk which was a blessing with us sharing with a full-grown Great Dane who had no concept of 'personal space'.

My relationship with my dad was rocky in the beginning, only because we really didn't know each other, but we soon realized most of the tension was because we were so much alike. His wife, Suzanne, was very gracious welcoming me into their lives but Brianna was a little hesitant at first. She'd been an only child and was reluctant to share her dad with me but after numerous phone calls, texts and then visits, we became friends, then sisters. My life was blessed with so many things and today, I was going to marry the man who I'd loved from the day we met.

The minister stepped forward and began the ceremony. "Welcome friends, we have been invited here today to share with Ian and Averi a very important moment in their lives. In the time they have been together, their love and understanding of each other has grown and matured, and now they have decided to live their lives together as husband and wife. Who gives this woman to be married to this man?"

"Her family does," both of my dads said in unison. I stepped over to take Ian's hand and he whispered, "You look incredible."

The way he looked at me as he took my hand reminded me of the night he'd proposed. We'd just moved into our new place, and I stopped on the way home to grab some pizza since we were still unpacking and hadn't organized the kitchen yet. As I pulled into the space in front of our unit, I saw Tiny sitting by the steps, his leash tied to the railing. I looked around but didn't see Ian anywhere. When I got closer, I saw a note pinned to his collar. I pulled it free and read it.

Tiny and I are playing hide-n-seek. Take his leash and let him try to find me.

I had to laugh. I knew this wasn't much of a game since Tiny could pick him out on a crowded beach and had done so a few times but I figured, why not. Holding the pizza out of the way of the snuffling nostrils attached to my big baby, I set it on the porch then took his leash and said, "Where's your daddy?"

He took off, dragging me down the sidewalk and around the building, his nose stuck to the ground. I was trying to keep up and not lose my flip flops when suddenly he stopped. He looked around from left to right then took off again. We'd gone about two blocks when I realized we were near a park. Tiny stopped again, let out a huge woof then sat down. Confused, I looked around but couldn't see anything. I heard a whistle, and Tiny took off yanking the leash from my hand. "Tiny!" I yelled chasing after him. It was starting to get dark, and I didn't want to lose him!

He ran straight to the gazebo and as I got closer, I discovered he wasn't alone. The gazebo was awash in candlelight and the sound of Keith Urban singing "Memories of Us". The floor was covered in rose petals and kneeling in the center beside Tiny, was Ian. Stunned, I climbed the steps. "What--" I stammered.

"Averi, as you've probably guessed by now, this isn't a game. I love you with every breath that I breathe, with every beat of my heart. My dream is that you'll share your life with me and make me the happiest man on earth. Will you marry me?" Pulling a ring box from behind his back, he opened it to reveal a beautiful platinum diamond ring.

Taking a deep breath, I said, "Ian, I love you too and I *will* marry you." The tears flowed freely as I watched him slide the ring onto my finger. "It's gorgeous!" I gasped.

"It's an Argyle diamond," he said kissing my hand. "It had to be different, just like you." The diamond had an unusual deep pink hue, and it was surrounded with classic diamonds and baguettes mirrored on both sides.

He pulled me close and kissed me to seal the promise of all the love we were going to share in our lives.

My thoughts were interrupted when I heard my name. "Ian and Averi, you are blessed to be here today surrounded by family and friends who wish to share in your special day. Let us pray."

Quickly handing my bouquet to Kendall, I took Ian's hand again. The minister led us in a prayer then signaled for the rings. We heard a loud woof and Tiny, who now weighed a whopping one hundred and seventy pounds, came down the aisle dragging Ian's friend Wyatt and our black Great Dane puppy, Sable behind him. They both had purple ribbons tied to their collars and attached to those were our rings. Ian slipped them from the ribbons, gave them both a treat and handed the rings to the minister. Wyatt was finally able to get Tiny to sit beside him but Sable insisted on sitting in his lap, much to the amusement of the guests.

The minister cleared his throat then continued, "For thousands of years, lovers have exchanged rings as a token of their vows. These rings are a sign that love has a past, a present, and a future. The promises which you've made to each other today will be forever in your hearts, but words are carried away with the wind so those who wear rings declare their love and commitment to each other. These rings announce to the world that you have found your soul mate," he said holding the rings aloft.

He handed my ring to Ian and said, "Ian, take Averi's ring, place it on her finger and repeat after me:

I give you this ring as a sign that I choose you and as a reminder that I will always love you.

To be my lover, my partner and my best friend, to the end of my days

Wear it, think of me, and know that I love you." He slipped my ring onto my finger then pressed his lips to it.

The minister then took Ian's ring and handed it to me. Averi, take Ian's ring, place it on his finger and repeat after me:

I give you this ring as a sign that I choose you and as a reminder that I will always love you.

To be my lover, my partner and my best friend, to the end of my days

Wear it, think of me, and know that I love you."

The minister continued. "In honor of Ian's father Patrick, I will now give them a traditional Irish Blessing."

"May your mornings bring joy and your evenings bring peace.

May your troubles grow few as your blessings increase.

May the saddest day of your future

Be no worse than the happiest day of your past.

May your hands be forever clasped in friendship

And your hearts joined forever in love.

Your lives are very special,

God has touched you in many ways.

May his blessings rest upon you

And fill all your coming days."

There was a chorus of amens and then the minister pronounced us husband and wife. When we kissed, it was supposed to be a quick one but Ian held me and wouldn't let me go. We finally broke apart when there were whistles and shouts for us to get a room. Hands clasped, we walked down the aisle accompanied by Carrie Underwood's "Ever, Ever After" and our guests' applause, but suddenly, when we got to the end of the carpet, Ian stopped. "What's wrong?" I asked. In one swoop, he picked me up and threw me over his shoulder. "Ian!" I laughed. "What are you doing?"

With a swat to my rear, he shouted, "I AM THE BEST MAN!"